Andrew Matthews

Andew Matthews was born in Barry, South Wales, in 1948. He lives in Reading with his wife, Sheena, and their cats. He taught English in Yateley School for many years before becoming a full-time writer in 1994. He has written many books for teenagers and younger readers. His hobbies include reading, listening to music and playing the guitar (badly). He hates travelling but likes being places. When he is nervous, he makes silly jokes. All the nice characters in his stories are based on real people – the nasty, irresponsible ones are made up.

Contents

STIKS & STOANS

Andrew Matthews

mammoth

for Helen and Joanne, who've been there
and for Miriam, who cares

First published in Great Britain in 1999 by Mammoth
an imprint of Egmont Children's Books Limited
239 Kensington High Street, London W8 6SA

Text copyright © 1999 Andrew Matthews
Cover illustration copyright © 1999 Jessica Meserve

The moral rights of the author and cover illustrator
have been asserted

ISBN 0 7497 3784 0

10 9 8 7 6 5 4 3 2

A CIP catalogue record for this title
is available from the British Library

Typeset by Avon Dataset Ltd, Bidford on Avon, B50 4JH
Printed in Great Britain by Cox & Wyman Ltd, Reading, Berkshire

Thay did it agein todae. Mrs Lynn toald them to stop but they havent stopt. They jest goe on doeing it orl the tiem. Thay goe on and on and on. I doant think thayll evre stop. Thay corl me naems liek TREE-TRUNK LEGS and ELLA FANT. They reackon Im thick. But Im not thick. Im a bit slow liek the docter says. I dident wont to goe in no specail neads class but I got put in thier anywae. Orl the kids in the class muck aruond and maek noies. You carnt hardley haer yourslef think somtiems. Miss Eves dose her best but thay doant listern. Thay reackon she is to soft.

My wrost enmey is that Billy Pickt. Billy Pickt is alwaes goeing on. He larfs at me. He corls me naems in the plaegrownd. I haet him. If I was a boye I woud smak him oen in the gob. He corls me THICKIE and I goe NO MY NAEM IS HICKIE NOT THICKIE but he jest larfs. It maeks me mad. I doant maen to get mad but I carnt help it. I crie wen I get mad. Billy Pickett larfs wen I crie. He leiks it wen I crie. I doant no why he dose it.

1

I doant no why poeple corl me naems. I wish thay woudent. I wish thay woud laeve me aloan. I nevre doen nothing to them. I nevre doen nothing to none.

Wen its bad I rember Nanna. Nanna was loevlie. Orl warm liek an ovne. She use to say STIKS AND STOANS MAE BRAEK MY BOANS BUT NAEMS WILL NEVRE HERT ME.

Prologue

Right at the last minute, Liam thought that he'd change his mind. He was going to take the lift back down to the ground floor and walk away, dump the flowers in the nearest bin, or give them to his mum. But when the lift doors opened, something pushed him outside, along the corridor and into the ward.

He spotted Ella straight away. Her plastered leg was suspended on wires from a metal frame. As Liam walked towards her, she turned her head, noticed him, and Liam got the bad-dream, this-can't-be-happening feeling. He stopped at the side of the bed, not knowing how to start.

Ella stared at him. 'Hello.'

'Hello,' said Liam.

'You're Liam, aren't you?'

Surprise made Liam laugh, and then he blushed because the laugh made him feel guilty. 'I didn't know you knew my name.' He held up the flowers. 'These are for you.'

They'd looked all right when he bought them; now he saw they were too bright: yellow, pink, orange and purple – colours that didn't go together.

'Oh, they're lovely! They're really lovely! You shouldn't of.'

There was nowhere to put the flowers – the top of Ella's bedside cabinet was crowded with get-well cards – so Liam lay them on the bed. 'How are you?'

'My leg's driving me mad,' said Ella. 'I can't get at it to itch it.'

'How long before the plaster comes off?'

'I dunno. I don't like to ask.'

Liam hadn't seen Ella so close before. She was nothing like the other Ella, the one who'd been in his head. Now he saw greeny-grey eyes, dreamy-looking. She was quite pretty in a plump, freckly sort of way.

'Why d'you come to see me?' Ella's voice wasn't hostile, just curious.

Here it was: what Liam had come to say, the part he'd been dreading. He couldn't talk to her eyes, so he lowered his head and gazed at the bedspread. 'I was there. The night it happened. I was one of them.'

'I know you was.'

Liam looked up, startled.

'I seen you in the bushes. You shouted for me to watch out, didn't you?'

'I think so.'

Ella's eyes clouded. 'I don't remember nothing what happened after that. I don't remember nothing till I woke up in hospital. It's like a bit's gone missing.'

Liam started to cry. He hadn't meant to and had no idea that he was going to, but suddenly hot tears were spilling out of his eyes. 'I'm sorry! I'm sorry! I'm sorry!' He went on saying it until his voice trailed off in a whisper.

'Shush! Shush now! I'll be all right. I'm going to get better.'

'It was just – like – a laugh. I didn't think . . . I didn't mean . . .'

'I know. It wasn't you. It was that Billy Pickett. He was the one. Don't get all upset, or you'll start me off.'

Liam sniffed, bit his bottom lip. He felt like he had a nail sticking in his throat. 'I wish I could take it back. I wish I could change what happened.'

'If wishes were horses, then beggars would ride,' said Ella. She smiled. 'My nanna used to say that. She was always saying stuff like that.' And then, because she could tell that the flowers and the tears weren't enough for Liam, Ella said, 'Will you do something for me?'

'What?'

'There's a book in my cupboard-thing. Will you get it for me?'

The book was the same size as a school exercise-book. On the front cover was a picture of a spaniel puppy, huge-eyed and thick-pawed, and so girly that it was embarrassing.

Liam held the book out to Ella, but she shook her head. 'You take it. It's my diary. I want you to read it.'

'Why?'

'So's you'll know. So's you'll understand. People don't really understand. I wouldn't let no one else read it but you.'

Underneath her freckles, Ella's face was turning pink, and it dawned on Liam that she was trusting him, asking him to be her friend. 'I'll read it,' he said.

'Will you come and see me again, after?'

'Yes. D'you want me to bring you anything when I do?'

Ella thought for a while, then said, 'Any magazine what's got a picture in it of Billy off of *Neighbours*.'

It took a long time for Liam to get up the nerve to open Ella's diary and when he did, he got a shock. Her hand-writing was part infant school printing, part joined-up. Some of the letters were reversed, the rest looked like they were part of a code and there wasn't a punctuation mark in sight.

I can't read this! thought Liam, but then a line in heavy block capitals jumped out at him.

STIKS AND STOANS MAE BRAEK MY BOANS BUT NAEMS WILL NEVRE HERT ME.

'Sticks and stones may break my bones, but names will never hurt me,' Liam said softly.

He went back to the top of the page, and tried. It was tough going at first, but gradually he got used to Ella's writing and began to hear her voice. Then it was *really* tough going, because it brought back all the stuff he'd tried to forget, all the stuff he'd tried to pretend about. Now he couldn't escape it.

Liam held his breath as his mind flooded with memories that were so deep he thought he was going to drown in them.

Ella's Diary

I never kept no diary before. I never thought about writing no diary, because writing is hard and I make lots of mistakes when I do it. But I don't suppose it matters if I make mistakes when no one is going to read it but myself. I'll know what it means.

I got the idea for the diary from Mr Clark. Mr Clark helps me with my English. Mr Clark says that if sometimes you have a big feeling about something and you write it down, it's a good way of letting your feelings out. I got plenty of big feelings. Sometimes they are so big I feel like I'm going to explode. So I am going to write down all about stuff that happens to me, just to see if it makes me feel any better.

I picked this book to write in because I like the puppy picture on the front. The puppy looks sweet. What I'm going to write about isn't sweet, but the puppy is. I wish I had a puppy to love.

They did it again today. Mrs Lynn told them to stop, but they haven't stopped. They just go on doing it all the time. They go on and on. I don't think they'll ever stop. They call me names like TREE-TRUNK LEGS and ELLA FANT. They reckon I'm thick, but I'm not thick. I'm a bit slow, like the doctor says. I didn't want to go in no Special Needs class, but I got put in there anyway. All the kids in the class muck around and make noise. You can't hardly hear yourself think sometimes. Miss Eaves does her best but they don't listen. They reckon she is too soft.

My worst enemy is that Billy Pickett. Billy Pickett is always going on. He laughs at me. He calls me names in the playground. I hate him. If I was a boy I would smack him one, right in the gob. He calls me THICKIE and I goes NO, MY NAME IS HICKIE, NOT THICKIE but he just laughs. It makes me mad. I don't mean to get mad, but I can't help it. I cry when I get mad. Billy Pickett laughs when I cry. He likes it when I cry. I don't know why he does it. I don't know why people call me names. I wish they wouldn't. I wish they would leave me alone. I never done nothing to them. I never done nothing to no one.

When it's bad, I remember Nanna. Nanna was lovely, all warm like an oven. She used to say, Sticks and stones may break my bones, but names will never hurt me. I wish Nanna was here to give me a cuddle, but she died. At her funeral, they put her in a box in a big hole in the ground. The earth and stones rattled on the box when they filled in the hole. That made me cry. I couldn't imagine my nanna in a box in the ground, all cold and alone. I go to her grave sometimes. I put flowers on the grave and talk to her. Sometimes I imagine I can hear her talking back to me. I miss her. I wish she wasn't dead. I get cuddles from Mum, but it's not the same as Nanna. Dad says I'm too big to cuddle now. I wish I wasn't. When I was little it was all right. No one hated me then. The other children used to play with me, and Nanna said I was her little sunbeam. I seen pictures of me when I was little, and I'm all smiling. I don't smile no more. I just cry.

Sometimes I think I am made of tears.

One

Liam dived for the bathroom as soon as he felt the cold tide dragging at his insides, and only just made it to the loo. He hated having the squits at the best of times, and this wasn't the best of times. All day he'd be worried about getting them again; it was one more thing he didn't need.

Liam flushed the loo and braced himself for the shower. He still hadn't got the hang of it. He could scald or freeze himself, but he couldn't get the temperature just right. He couldn't get anything in the new house right: he reached for door handles that weren't there, clutched nothing when he went to grab the light cord in the bathroom. His bedroom felt as uncomfortable as a twisted sock. The window was on the wrong side of the bed; the wardrobe stood against the wrong wall.

And the house sounded strange: the cistern of the loo

made a weird whistling noise as it filled; the fridge-freezer in the kitchen buzzed; there were bumps on the landing late at night. Liam was afraid that the house might be haunted, but when he mentioned his fear to Mum, she laughed and said, 'I wish. We could charge people for guided tours if it was.'

One thing the new house had going for it, though – total absence of Dad. There were no memories for Liam to run into.

New house, new town, new school. It was the new school that gave Liam the squits. He'd been shown around just before the holidays and come away totally bewildered by the kaleidoscope of buildings and the muffled roar of eighteen hundred pupils migrating between lessons. Now he had to go back for real, and he was convinced that he wouldn't be able to get through the first day without getting lost, told off and made a fool of.

Liam went to his bedroom to get dressed. The uniform sweater was dark blue, emblazoned with the Oxfield Comprehensive badge: a stylised bull's head above the motto *Docendo discemus* which, according to the school handbook, meant *We learn by teaching*. The tie was dark red with blue diagonal stripes. Before Liam went downstairs he checked himself out in the wardrobe mirror. The uniform screamed, 'New Kid!' He had the eyes of a small, furry animal about to enter an environment where everything ate small, furry animals. It was all his parents' fault. Their marriage had fallen apart and he was the one who was suffering for it. Things had changed so fast that the ghost of the person he used to be was still hanging in the air. His world, once safe and cosy, was full of spikes.

Mum was standing in the kitchen, eating breakfast: half a slice of unbuttered toast and a cup of weak tea without milk or sugar. She was wearing her charcoal-grey trouser suit and smelled of shampoo and perfume. 'You look smart.'

Liam grunted. Smart was the worst; he would have given anything to look ordinary, to look like he fitted in.

'You must be excited.'

'More like terrified.'

Mum gave him one of her eyes-closed smiles, dealing with the problem the way she usually dealt with a problem – by pretending that it didn't exist. 'You'll be fine. It's bound to be a bit strange at first, but you'll soon get used to it.'

Liam grunted again.

'What are you going to have for breakfast?'

'Nothing. I'm not hungry.'

Mum frowned. 'You must eat something, Liam. You can't go to school on an empty stomach.'

'Then I'll have to go on the bus.'

Mum didn't react. She either didn't get the joke, or didn't think it was funny.

Liam took a bowl from the overhead cupboard and shook cornflakes into it. They looked like autumn leaves.

'When I drop you off, go straight to reception. You remember where that is, don't you?'

'Uh-hu.'

'Ask the receptionist for Mr Cooper.'

'Uh-hu.'

'And wait for me in reception at the end of school. I shouldn't be later than four.'

Liam doubted it. Mum was always late. She estimated time by hope, not experience. 'There's no need to drive me home. I can walk it. It's not that far.'

'I don't want you to walk, not for the first week, anyway. I don't want you wandering the streets.'

'I wouldn't wander the streets. I'd come straight home.'

'You're not too big for me to meet you from school.'

She was treating him as if he were five, not twelve. She didn't want to let him out of her sight. He'd be labelled as a Mummy's Boy and get picked on.

Mummy's Boy, New Kid, Outsider; any label would do.

Reception was like a disturbed ants'-nest. Kids streamed past, climbing the slope of the wheelchair ramp, passing through the fire doors into the branching corridors beyond. There was a strong start-of-term feeling, like the school was a well-shaken can of fizzy drink.

The receptionist was hassled. Every time she put down the phone it rang again. Liam stood at the counter, waiting for her to finish. He knew the passing kids were staring at him and he tried not to notice; if he blushed, he was dead.

The receptionist put her hand over the mouthpiece of the phone and said, 'Sorry about this. Shan't be a moment,' but the phone went on ringing and she went on answering it.

Teachers arrived, cruising through reception like sharks, grim-mouthed and cold-eyed. Some smiled at the receptionist and wiggled their fingers in a wave, then their smiles snapped off. A tall man with receding hair and a grizzled beard gave Liam a sharp glance and approached cautiously, as though Liam were a firework that had failed to go off. The man said, 'Are you Liam Noakes?'

'Yes, sir.'

'I'm Mr Cooper. You're in my form.'

'Eight Luke West.'

Mr Cooper grinned. 'Eight Luke before you leap. Never go into the form room without a chair, a whip and a revolver.'

'Sir?' said Liam, alarmed.

'Only joking, Liam. They're not bad – not by Oxfield Comp standards. There are times I could swear they were almost human. D'you know where the form room is?'

'No, sir.'

'Pity. I was hoping you could tell me.' Mr Cooper pointed to a bench near the entrance doors. 'Sit over there. I'll collect you after the staff meeting.' His eyes turned sympathetic. 'Nervous?'

'Yes, sir.'

'That makes two of us,' said Mr Cooper.

Liam was put in the care of Harry Watson. Harry had flaky pale skin, pale eyes and pale lashes that he blinked slowly. A vein on his left temple showed like a blue worm, or a river on a map. His voice was wheezy; he sucked at an inhaler.

Mr Cooper finished the register and said, 'Listen up, Eight LW. As those of you who are awake will have noticed, Liam has joined us this morning.'

Faces turned to look; Liam let his eyes go out of focus.

Mr Cooper said, 'You know how he feels, because you were new to the school last year. Be gentle with him. No practical jokes. Show him how considerate and responsible you can be. If you don't, I'll rip your right arms off and beat you round the head with the soggy ends. Now I want you to fill in the fronts of your pristine homework logs. A certain amount of chat is permitted.'

There was a low buzz of conversation.

Harry said, 'He's all right, Mr Cooper is.'

Liam nodded.

'We got English first lesson. Mrs Field. She's all right too. After that we got maths with Mr Marsh.'

'Is he all right?'

'No. He's power-mad. If your homework's untidy he makes you do it again.'

'What's the school like?'

The question fazed Harry. 'It's like . . . you know . . . school. Prison.'

'What are the other kids in the form like?'

'Mostly all right, apart from Billy Pickett and that lot.'

'Which one's Billy Pickett?'

'The kid with the dark hair and goggly eyes, two tables to the right. Him and his mates keep giving me grief because of my hobby.'

Liam expected Harry to go on, but he didn't, so Liam asked, 'What hobby's that?'

'I keep seahorses. In a tank with water. Salt water, like seawater, you know. It's the males that give birth. They're very relaxing. I like to watch them swimming around. It takes my mind off of things. They don't do much. It's interesting.'

There was a lot more, but Liam switched off. He wasn't looking forward to being stuck with Harry for the rest of the week. He'd been hoping they might make friends, but there was nothing to make friends with. Liam realised that Harry didn't get grief because he kept seahorses, he got grief because he was Harry.

Two

When the bell went at the end of lesson two, Harry said, 'It's break now. We don't have to go to next lesson for another fifteen minutes. We can go outside.'

Harry needed to explain things, to make sure nothing had changed while he wasn't looking. He was so irritating; Liam knew that by the end of the day he'd be daydreaming about shoving Harry under a bus.

It was sunny outside, but a cold wind gusted around the campus. Spring had begun in February, now it was April and the weather was turning frosty. Liam wondered what had happened to global warming.

Several games of football were being played on the netball courts across the way. Year seven kids chased one another in a nameless game that involved a lot of shouting. Languid-eyed year ten girls were failing to be impressed by year ten boys.

Liam and Harry perched on a low wall outside Newton Block, where they'd just had maths. Harry took a polythene box out of his sports bag, prised off the lid and removed a KitKat. He carefully pushed the KitKat out of its paper collar, turned it over and picked at the foil with his fingernails. When the foil opened, Harry neatly folded it back all the way around until the first finger of chocolate was uncovered.

Liam watched, fascinated. 'D'you always eat KitKats like that?' he said.

'Like what?' said Harry.

'Tidily.'

Harry frowned. 'What's wrong with being tidy?' he said.

'Nothing.'

'I like to undo my KitKat slowly. All the time I'm doing it, I think about what it's going to taste like.'

'It's going to taste like a KitKat, isn't it?'

The words fell out of Liam's mouth before he could stop them.

Harry didn't seem offended, or maybe the sarcasm had gone right over his head. 'KitKats aren't always the same. I had one once where the biscuit was nearly burnt. And another one I had didn't have no biscuit in it at all. It was just, like, chocolate all the way through.'

'Really?'

'Yeah. I expect they made a mistake at the factory.'

Liam, desperate to snap the iron links of Harry's logic, began making up stuff. 'My dad can nibble all the chocolate off the outside of a Crunchie. He can nibble all the chocolate off a Mars, and the toffee layer, so it's a Milky Way with no clothes on.'

'What's he want to do that for?' asked Harry.

'For fun. For a game. Have you ever sucked a Polo till it's really, really thin and then put it over one of your pointy teeth and wobbled it round? It feels like your tooth's falling out, doesn't it?'

Harry's eyes were troubled. 'I don't like it when my teeth fall out. I used to be frightened of the Tooth Fairy when I was little. And Father Christmas. I didn't like how they were supposed to be able to get in your room when you were asleep. I had nightmares about it.'

'When I was six, my dad took me to Lapland to see Father Christmas. We had to ride in this sleigh pulled by reindeer. Father Christmas lived in a log cabin in the middle of a pine forest. On the way back, we heard wolves howling.'

All rubbish; Liam didn't know why he was doing it – Harry wasn't worth the bother.

'I expect it was some bloke dressed up as Father Christmas, like in those big department stores.'

'Yeah. It was good going to Lapland, though.'

'I don't like going places. I'd rather stay home.'

Liam thought it was incredible that there was so much he and Harry didn't have in common. 'It must be a pain having me trailing around after you.'

Harry shrugged. 'Don't mind.'

'You don't have to nursemaid me. I mean, if you'd rather go off and find your friends . . .'

'Not really,' said Harry, not taking the hint.

Another voice said, 'What goes clip-clop, clip-clop, splash?'

Liam turned his head. Billy Pickett was leaning over the white fence around the raised forecourt of Newton Block. Mockery flickered in his eyes, like light on water. His thin lips were twisted into a half smile.

Harry looked, scowled, turned his head away.

Billy said, 'Hey, Watson telly! What goes clip-clop, clip-clop, splash?'

Liam got it and laughed. The laugh earned him a glance from Billy: down, up, gone. Billy was estimating how much of a threat Liam might be.

'How would I know?'

'D'you play water polo with them seahorses of yours? How d'you get them to keep still while you put their saddles on?'

'Ha, ha, ha. When I first heard that one, I laughed until I fell off my dinosaur.' Harry put what was left of the KitKat back into the polythene box, replaced the box in the sports bag and stood up. 'You coming?' he said to Liam.

'In a minute. You go on. I'll catch you up. I've got some stuff I need to get sorted.'

Another lie. Harry knew it was a lie this time, knew that Liam didn't want him around. He walked off, puffing.

Liam looked at Billy and saw that Billy was the one. People who got on the wrong side of Billy Pickett were given a hard time. It showed in Billy's face, in the way he tilted back his head to look down his long nose, in the way he said, 'You're that new kid, aren't you?'

'I'm Liam Noakes, and I'm mad!' Liam did the thing with his eyes that made them spin like the eyes of a cartoon character who'd been hit on the head.

Billy laughed. 'Are you cracked, or what?'

'I'm loopier than Mr Loopy's Fruity Loops.' Liam sang the Fruity Loops jingle; Billy joined in and they sang the last line together.

Billy knew that Liam was putting on an act for his benefit and felt flattered. Maybe Liam was good for a laugh; maybe he wasn't as big a plonker as he looked. Billy said, 'What d'you reckon to Harry, then?'

'Personality-free zone,' said Liam.

'He told you about his seahorses yet?'

'In detail. I had to stick needles in my arm to keep

awake. He could bore for England, couldn't he?'

'If boring was in the Olympics, he'd get given a gold medal,' said Billy.

'If they paid people to be boring, Harry could turn professional.' Liam felt a twinge of guilt: Harry had only tried to be helpful, but putting him down was building Liam up in Billy's eyes.

'What football team d'you support?' Billy said it casually, but Liam knew it was a question about tribal loyalty.

Liam had worked out an answer well in advance, knowing that somebody was bound to ask him sooner or later. 'Dundee United.'

Billy's face wrinkled up. 'Uh? But they're *Scottish*.'

'I know. I'm into the Scottish Premier League. My dad's Scottish. He takes me to see Dundee United sometimes. Fantastic atmosphere.'

'Which English side d'you support?'

Liam swayed this way and that, as though he were being pulled in opposite directions. 'I don't know. There are too many good sides. Scottish football's easier to follow.'

'My best teams are Chelsea and Man United.'

'Yeah. Man United are cool.'

It made the spite go out of Billy's face.

A bell rang.

Billy groaned and rolled his eyes. 'Double art with Mrs Unwin. She doesn't half go on.' His face changed: his nose sharpened, his chin softened, his voice became a fruity sing-song. 'Think *form*, children! Think *colour*!'

Liam hadn't met Mrs Unwin, but he guessed that Billy's imitation of her was spot-on. He bet that Billy practised impersonations on his own, and didn't show them to anybody until he had them off perfect.

'Know where the art room is?'

'No. Harry was going to show me.'

'You can come with me, if you like.'

And Liam knew that he'd passed the test.

Ella's Diary

I got this thing I didn't want and it's not my fault, because I was born with it in me. I didn't know nothing about it till I done this test thing they gave me to do at my other school, and after I done the test thing they told me I got it. It is called dys-. I don't know the rest. I can't put the rest. I don't like it, having a thing I can't put. Mrs Lynn says it makes me special, which is why I got to be in Special Needs so I can do things my way, at my own speed. But all the kids say that Special Needs is for people who are divvy and that. But I am not no divvy. Things just take me a bit longer.

First it was funny tonight and then it wasn't. It was funny when me and Dad and Mum was watching Coronation Street, and Dad done this really loud windy-poop, and Mum goes, 'Cor, Joe! What you been eating? It smells like something crawled up your backside and died.'

And Dad goes, 'Well I haven't eaten nothing but what you

made, so it's your fault. You better open some windows so we can breathe.'

We were all like laughing because Dad done it so loud. It was funny, not rude. Nanna used to say that there wasn't nothing rude but like in your mind. Like in some people's minds, all ordinary stuff is rude. I reckon Billy Pickett got a mind like that.

Then we stopped laughing. It wasn't funny no more because the phone rang and Mum went to answer it, but when she answered it there wasn't no one there. It went again and again, and again, on and on and on. And it wasn't no one. I got frightened. It was creepy to think someone would ring and not say nothing. I got to thinking it must be kids from school. I think it's not enough for them to do stuff to me at school. I think they want to do it when I'm home as well. I feel like a mouse feels when there is this big cat waiting for it outside its hole, and it can't go nowhere or do nothing but just stay all frightened, with its eyes and whiskers all trembly silver, thinking about the cat's sharp teeth and claws. Nothing safe. Nowhere to go. Nothing to do but be scared all the time.

At school they say I am big and fat, but I'm not. I'm small. I'm the smallest mouse ever.

Three

Mum lasted until Wednesday before she stopped meeting Liam from school. She said she was sorry, but the office was chasing a big contract and everybody had to put in extra hours. Liam knew she meant that she'd seen a chance to suck up to her new boss by working late to show how keen she was. Mum had always done that. It had been one of the things that she and Dad used to row about. Once in a while Dad would complain that it wasn't right for Liam to be left at a friend's house, or with a childminder, and Mum would tell him that she had a career to think about, and if he was so worried about Liam why didn't *he* come home early for a change.

Liam wondered why they'd had him, when he was such an inconvenience to them.

It didn't matter about Mum not picking him up from school. It took pressure off Liam and gave him more time to get to know Billy Pickett and his mates, gave them more time to get to know the Liam he wanted them to think he was. He'd decided that wacky was the way to go, weird but harmless. While they were laughing at him, Liam was making mental recordings, sussing things out.

Billy was interesting; charmingly dangerous. When he took the mickey out of people he did it with his down-the-nose stare, eyes hooded, voice a low drawl, like thinking up a put-down was no bother and there were plenty more where that one came from. As far as Billy was concerned the other members of Eight Luke West were targets, and they were wary of him. Some tried to join in, some pretended to ignore what Billy said, but they all got twitchy when they were around him. Billy was Bad Boy, Mr Attitude, the one the teachers either hassled or left well alone.

Billy's mates, Des and Bing, revolved around him like minor moons.

Des was tall and gangly, with milk-chocolate brown skin and fleecy black hair, cut short. He told jokes about West Indians and himself, putting himself down for being black before anyone else did.

Bing's real name was Simon, and he didn't explain how he got his nickname. Bing was stocky, mousey-haired. His left eye was lazy, the lid drooping in a frozen wink. He was slow, clumsy, bear-like. Billy enjoyed winding Bing up and Bing took it, grinning, eyes burning with suppressed anger. If anyone else had said what Billy said, Bing would have flattened them, but he was cowed by Billy's sharp tongue: everybody was.

After school on Thursday, Liam walked home for the first time. Billy and Bing came part of the way, then Bing peeled off and it was just Billy and Liam.

Billy said, 'Got a computer?'

'Yeah,' said Liam. Dad had bought it for him, just before he walked out. Top-of-the-range PC: stereo speakers, hundred quid joystick, a grand's worth of software. Liam spent more time with it than he ever had with Dad.

'On the Net?' said Billy.

'Course.'

'Cool! I've got this really excellent shoot 'em up. *Carnage Castle*. Plenty of blood and guts. Dead tasty. I'll let you download it if you want. We could have a game together.'

'I've already got it. Top game, right?' Actually Liam thought it was tacky and had stopped playing it because it was so boring.

'What level d'you get to?'

'All the way.'

Billy scowled. 'Get outta here! The only way you can

get past the vampires is if you know the cheat.'

'Nope. If you look in the Necromancer's cauldron, you find a stash of silver bullets to kill the vampires with. Then you use the golden key to open the last door.'

'What happens then?'

'This manky page comes up for you to register for extra levels. And you get a map to design your own corridors.'

'That it?'

'Pretty much.'

'Huh! Not as good as *Pyramid Plunder*. When you finish that, Dusti Newlands gets her kit off. Phwoar!'

'Phwoar!' Liam didn't have the faintest idea what Billy was talking about.

'Great bazoomas! Hey, you seen Heather Bond in Nine Matthew South? She's got plenty up top, hasn't she?'

'If she ran for the bus, she'd knock herself out,' said Liam.

'No chance of her drowning in the pool.'

They laughed raucously to show each other that they'd got it.

'So what d'you reckon? You up for a session of *Carnage* tonight?'

'Def,' said Liam. 'About seven?'

'What's wrong with as soon as we get in?'

'Homework. My mum checks to see I've done it.'

Billy curled his top lip. 'You want to get her properly trained, mate. My old dear signs the homework log without bothering to read it. Homework's a waste of time. We wouldn't have to do any if the teachers taught us properly at school.'

'You know teachers. They invented homework because they couldn't stand to think of us enjoying ourselves in our spare time.'

Billy turned into Mr Marsh – he even looked like he had glasses on. In Mr Marsh's voice, Billy said, 'Your homework is to complete exercise seven and exercise eight, and make sure that you do them very, very neatly.'

Liam giggled. 'That's brilliant! How d'you do that?'

Billy shrugged with one shoulder. 'Just talk like you've got an ice pop up your bum.'

Billy lived in Dryden Crescent. He left Liam at the corner. Liam waited to see if Billy would give him a final wave, but he didn't, so Liam walked on. He was thinking about his homework. He always did homework as soon as he got in so that the lessons would still be fresh in his mind, and to get it out of the way so that it wouldn't be hanging over him for the rest of the evening. Liam wanted to do well at school, but he didn't want to stand out too much, or he'd get branded as a suck.

On the last stretch of the journey home, Liam passed the Butts, a lumpy field fenced in with an iron railing.

Kids played there after school and at weekends, adults used it to exercise their dogs, teenagers went there at night to get out of it on cider and blow. As he walked by, Liam vaguely registered somebody on the other side of the railing, but he didn't pay any attention until he got the crawly feeling between his shoulder blades that meant someone was watching him. He turned and caught a girl staring at him.

She was dumpy, overweight. She had straw-coloured, chin-length hair and her round face was crowded with freckles. When Liam made eye contact with her she blushed, wheeled around and lumbered away, shifting her weight from leg to leg as if she were pacing the deck of a ship caught in a heavy swell.

There was something sad about her. Liam could tell that she was depressed from the sag of her shoulders and the way her head was lowered in a permanent cringe.

He was glad that he didn't feel the way she looked.

There was a message from Mum on the answerphone. She wasn't going to be home before eight; microwave dinner in the freezer. The message ended, 'I'm a terrible mother, aren't I? I'll make it up to you, I promise.'

Liam grimaced, thinking he wouldn't hold his breath.

Liam and Billy played *Carnage Castle* as a duo, plundering

secret compartments for nail guns and grenade launchers, offing hellhounds, armoured guards and ghouls until the walls dripped virtual blood. They made a good team, watching each others' backs. In the game, Billy was a barrel-chested hunk, square-jawed and narrow-eyed, wearing combat fatigues with the sleeves torn off the top to reveal impossibly well-developed biceps.

When the game was finished, Liam typed: *Another go?*

Billy wrote back: *Head to head?*

He might as well have used an exclamation mark; it wasn't a question.

You're on, Liam wrote. *You hide, I'll come looking for you.*

Electronic hide-and-seek, except when you found your mates you didn't call them out, you blew them apart with a scatter-gun.

Liam knew just where Billy would choose to conceal himself: in the labyrinth of the dungeon cesspit, where it was difficult to get a clear shot because of all the slime-encrusted pillars. There were loads of places for Billy to set up an ambush. Liam's character would have to pick his way carefully to avoid slipping into deep trenches and drowning.

But Liam had an edge that Billy didn't know about. In the suit of rusty armour that stood outside the labyrinth door was a miniaturised breathing apparatus that would allow Liam to swim underwater. He could sneak up on Billy and blast him from behind. It would be good – Liam's skill points would go off the scale and his cool rating would max-out.

Liam used the hand-shaped cursor to grasp the breathing apparatus and clicked on the door. It opened on shrieking hinges, warning Billy that he was coming. Liam swam slowly and methodically, finally making Billy out behind the pillar where the Super Ghoul usually lurked. Billy was a pair of legs, rippling to give a submerged effect. Liam went around the pillar, then stopped. Something was nagging at him like the pain of a splinter, and it took a couple of minutes to work out what it was.

He swam back to the door, stood up and waded through the gunge, making a good job of dodging from pillar to pillar, letting the barrel of his weapon stick out enough to show Billy where he was, without its being too obvious. At the end of the game, Liam took his finger off the fire-button and took a half-step into the open so that Billy could shoot him and win.

Billy wrote: *Your ass is grass. See ya, sucker.*

Liam wrote: *Get you next time* – and knew he wouldn't.

Mum got home at quarter to nine, glittery-eyed and giving off alcohol fumes. She said, 'I'm sorry I'm so late, darling. Paul asked me if I'd like to go for a drink, and I couldn't really say no.'

'Paul?' said Liam.

'My boss.'

Up until now, Mum's boss had been 'Mr Harben'. Liam noted the sudden familiarity and added it to his watch-for-danger signs list. Mum had already made noises about how good-looking her new boss was. She was always attracted to authority figures. Dad had started off as her boss.

'What have you been doing?'

'Homework,' said Liam, 'playing games on the Internet.'

'Oh?'

'With a friend from school.'

Mum's face lit up like a Christmas high street. 'See?' she said. 'You haven't been at school a week and you've already made friends. I told you it wouldn't take long for you to settle in.'

Liam smiled.

Ella's Diary

I went for a walk after school. I went down the Butts to be on my own. I like going down the Butts when I am feeling lonely. It's quiet there. I can be by myself. It's good when shadows come in the evening, 'cos no one can see me in the dark.

I seen a boy. I seen him before at school. He goes around with Billy Pickett and them, but he's nothing like Billy. Billy Pickett looks all creepy, like a rat. This boy doesn't look like a rat. He looks nice. He's got brown hair and brown eyes. I think he's got brown eyes. It was difficult to tell, because I wasn't very close to him. They are nice eyes, whatever colour they are. He is quite tall and his clothes are clean. He looks gentle and a bit shy. He looked at me and I got all hot. I wished I could say something to him, but I couldn't. I had to walk away. I looked through the bushes to see where he lives. It is a big house, bigger than ours. It would be nice to talk to someone like that boy, someone who was gentle. The only boys who talk to me are nasty. They say things to hurt.

The phone didn't ring tonight. I hope that means they are bored of their stupid game. It's not fair. Dad says nothing is fair. Nanna used to say that life is what you make it, but what happens when no one lets you make it anything?

When I am grown up and leave school, I am going away somewhere different, somewhere no one knows me. I will meet someone nice, and get married, and have babies, and I won't let no one say all nasty things to them. If they do, I'll go right up to their school and tell them to do something about it. They don't know how much it hurts. It is worse than having a pain. You can't get to it to make it better. It's a pain you can't touch. It's deep, deep down inside where everything is black. It's not nice having a black place inside where you have to keep going all the time. It sucks you in like water going down the plug-hole. I wonder if dying is like that, so you are sad for ever and ever? There is supposed to be a Heaven where everyone is happy. Hell is supposed to be all flames, but I don't think it is all flames. I think it is just black and alone, with no one to give you cuddles. But if it is like that, at least no one would go on at you all the time. You could get a minute's peace.

We had fish fingers for tea, and oven chips and peas. I had tomato sauce on mine.

I didn't laugh tonight. Nothing happened to make me laugh, just sad and down in the dumps.

That boy I saw, I wonder what his name is? I wonder what

he's doing, going round with Billy Pickett and them? Some boys are like that. They go round in gangs because they reckon it makes them look hard. They do stupid stuff to make each other laugh.

I wish something nice would happen to me tomorrow. I wish they would treat me like normal, and not like a freak.

Four

On Friday morning Bing had a black eye which wasn't so much black as purple, red and yellow. Liam saw it when he joined Eight Luke West outside the Shakespeare Block before the start of registration. Billy and Des were huddled protectively around Bing. Bing was turned in on himself. His skin was grey. He kept clenching and unclenching his fists.

'What happened to you, Bing?'

Bing didn't seem to hear.

Des said, 'Jealous of me, isn't he? He's trying to turn himself black but he can only do it a bit at a time.'

Liam laughed; Bing didn't, his jaw muscles bunched as he ground his teeth.

Billy looked *leave it* at Liam and said, 'Gave you a right stuffing last night, didn't I?'

'Certainly did. I didn't even know what hit me. I was

like –' Liam crossed his eyes, puffed out his cheeks, smacked the palm of his right hand against his forehead and staggered back.

'That's what you get for messing with me. I'm the King of *Carnage Castle*.'

All around them, people were glancing at Billy and muttering. Liam wondered what was going on.

'Saturday tomorrow. Great. Lie in, slob round watching telly all morning. What you doing tomorrow afternoon, Lee?'

Liam frowned, then twigged that *he* was Lee. The name meant that he was in. 'Not a lot. Going to the supermarket with my mum, I expect.'

'Thrills!' said Billy.

Liam backtracked quickly. 'I have to help her with the shopping because my dad's away. He's working in Saudi Arabia.'

'Yeah? What's he do, then?'

'Engineer,' Liam said. It was suitably vague.

Billy's face showed no interest. 'My dad's a lorry driver. Least he was when I last saw him, six months ago.'

'I don't know who my dad is,' Des said cheerfully.

Liam said, 'What's your dad, Bing?'

Bing's eyes flared. He spoke through clenched teeth. 'A bastard.'

Jamie Fergerson strolled over, smirking. He pointed

to Bing's black eye and said, 'Walk into another door, Bing?'

'I was playing with my little brother. We fell over and his elbow jabbed me in the eye.'

Bing's voice was expressionless. It was like he'd rehearsed the speech until he was word-perfect.

'Oh yeah?' said Jamie.

Billy said, 'Get lost, Fergersoff! If Bing says it was an accident, it was an accident, right? None of your business anyway.'

Jamie looked as if he were longing to say something else, but his nerve failed him and he went off to stand by himself.

The registration bell rang. Teachers drifted over from the staffroom and herded their forms in through the double doors. Mr Cooper was one of the last to arrive. He caught sight of Bing and frowned. 'Right, Eight Luke West,' he said, 'go into the form room and wait quietly while I have a word with Simon.'

From the windows of the form room, Liam could see Mr Cooper talking to Bing. Bing had his back turned to the windows. Mr Cooper's expression was serious. Liam couldn't hear what he was saying, but saw Bing's shoulders start to pump up and down. Mr Cooper reached out to put a hand on Bing's arm and Bing flinched away, shaking his head. Mr Cooper said something else and came inside. When Mr Cooper was out of sight, Bing turned and gave the wall a hard kick.

Liam looked away; he didn't feel he should watch any more; it was too private.

When the bell went at the end of last lesson, Liam felt a surge of relief. He'd survived his first week at Oxfield Comp and it hadn't been anything like as bad as he'd feared. He joined Billy, Des and Bing in the home-going tide. The current beached them on the pavement outside the school gates.

Des said to Billy, 'See you tomorrow, yeah? Outside the centre at half one?'

'Don't be late.'

Liam, Billy and Bing walked on.

Liam said, 'What centre was Des talking about?'

'St Mary's Centre in town,' said Billy. 'That mall opposite the big church, you know?'

'Right,' said Liam. He'd seen the mall but hadn't been inside. 'What d'you do there?'

'Hang out, have a laugh. You coming, Bing?'

'No.'

'Go on! We'll do the bus number. You'll be great at it with that eye.'

'I don't feel like it, OK?' Bing snapped.

'All right, all right, don't get your knickers in a knot,'

said Billy. His eyes suddenly changed and a grin spread across his face. 'Well, well, look who's coming,' he said, nudging Bing in the ribs. 'Miss Tree-Trunk Two Thousand.'

Liam followed Billy's gaze and saw the girl who'd been in the Butts. She glowered at Billy, death-rays beaming out of her eyes.

Bing chuckled. It was the happiest noise he'd made all day. 'Ella Thickie,' he said; he sounded as though he were speaking through a mouthful of chocolate.

'Get a load of those legs,' said Billy. 'All that meat and no veg.'

Bing sniggered; Liam smiled because he knew he was supposed to.

Billy raised his voice as the girl drew nearer and said, 'Hello, Ella. And how are you this afternoon?' His politeness was exaggerated, teasing.

Ella stopped walking and put her hands on her hips. Her face flushed crimson. 'Now don't you start on me, Billy Pickett. You leave me alone or I'll tell Mrs Lynn on you.'

Mrs Lynn was year eight head. Liam looked at Billy to see his reaction, so that he'd know how to react himself.

Billy went mock-offended. 'What you going to tell her, Ella? That I said hello? Ooh, I'm a naughty boy, aren't I?'

'I know what you do. You call me Tree-Trunk Legs and Thickie.'

Billy turned to Bing and Liam. 'Did I say that? Did you hear me say anything like that? You've got a persecution complex, Ella. You ought to go straight home and have a lie down.'

'Have to be a big bed,' Bing said softly.

Ella crossed the road to avoid further confrontation.

'Look at the backside on that,' Billy said. 'Looks like two pit bulls fighting in a sack, doesn't it?'

Bing said, 'Her bum's so big she got to go through her front door sideways.'

'She has to buy two tickets when she gets on the bus,' said Billy.

Liam laughed. 'Who is she?'

'That's Ella Thickie,' said Billy.

'Is that really her name?'

'Course not,' said Billy. 'Her real name's Hickie but we call her Thickie because she *is* a thicky. She's in Special Needs class with the rest of the dipsticks.'

Bing said, 'She's the only person I know who could form a group on her own.'

Liam said, 'Tough on her when they split up, though.'

'Don't mock the afflicted,' said Billy. 'She's going down the doctor's tonight.'

Liam knew it was a set-up and pretended that he

didn't. 'Is she? What's wrong with her?'

'Nothing,' said Billy. 'She just needs a new knicker prescription. Bungee rope snapped on her old pair.'

Bing cracked up and doubled over. Something he needed to get rid of was coming out in his laugh. Tears brimmed over his eyelids and tumbled down his face.

'He's gone,' said Billy.

Liam said, 'Hey, Bing? D'you reckon Ella gets her dresses from Rent-a-Tent? Know why she never goes swimming? She's afraid of being harpooned.' He was making himself laugh, as well as Bing. In his mind, Ella Thickie was just a cartoon character.

'They never let her in the pool, in case she floods the place,' said Billy.

Liam could see it: a vast Ella, looking nonplussed, sitting in an empty swimming pool, scratching her head while terrified staff and pupils fled from a gigantic tidal wave.

'No more!' Bing gasped. 'No more, or I'll wet meself!'

Billy did Ella. He seemed to swell up. He held out his arms and stamped his feet like a Sumo wrestler. 'Come on, big boy!' he said in a deep, slow voice. 'I'm all woman and I'm all yours!'

Bing collapsed on to the pavement.

Billy and Liam stood at the corner of Dryden Crescent.

Liam didn't want to go home yet, he wanted to stay with Billy, stacking joke on joke until the pile overbalanced; but Billy wasn't in a joking mood any more.

Billy said, 'Bing's black eye wasn't an accident. His dad gave it to him last night. His dad came home from the pub legless and started knocking his old woman about. Bing tried to stop him, and his dad clocked him one.'

'What?' said Liam.

'It's happened loads of times before. Bing's dad gets dead nasty after he's had a few.'

'Why didn't Bing call the police?'

'Doesn't want anyone to know, does he? He's afraid he'll get taken into care. Don't you say anything. If you blab it around, Bing'll break your face.'

'Why does his mum put up with it?' said Liam.

'Go figure,' Billy said. 'My old dear wouldn't. That's why she left. I stayed with my dad for a while, but . . .' He mimed sinking pints. 'Too much of that. Bad news. I couldn't handle it, so I went to live with my mum.'

There wasn't anything for Liam to say.

Billy said bitterly, 'I hope he drinks himself to death.'

Liam wanted to do something to lighten the atmosphere. He said, 'Look, about tomorrow afternoon, maybe I can talk my mum into doing the shopping on her own.'

Billy brightened. 'You reckon?'

'I can give it a go. Let me work on her and I'll give you a bell.'

'Whatever. Be cool if you could.'

Liam took a big breath and said, 'That stuff I told you about my dad? It wasn't true. He's not working abroad. He and Mum got divorced at Christmas.'

He hadn't admitted it to anyone before; it had taken a lot to come out with it.

'I know.'

Liam was gobsmacked. 'How?'

'The way you talked about your dad. I could tell you were lying.'

Mum was in by six. She said that Friday night was now officially pizza delivery night. After she phoned through the order, Liam said, 'Mum, is it all right if I go out with my friends tomorrow afternoon?'

'Of course it is. Where are you going?'

'Nowhere. Just into town.'

'Actually, that gets me out of a tricky situation. Paul asked me if I'd go into the office tomorrow afternoon to deal with some faxes we're expecting from the States. I was feeling guilty about leaving you on your own, but if you're going to be with your friends, you won't mind, will you?'

'Mm,' said Liam, knowing that Mum would have gone into the office whether he'd minded or not.

Ella's Diary

I seen that nice boy again after school. He was with Billy Pickett and his mates. He was laughing with them. I'm sure they was laughing at me, and he was just laughing to keep in with Billy.

BILLY PICKETT IS A PIG. HE'S A SWINE. HE COME OUT HIS MOTHER THE WRONG WAY AROUND.

I shouldn't think no bad thoughts about no one. Nanna used to say if you can't say nothing good about no one, you shouldn't say nothing at all. But I can't help it. Billy Pickett makes me have bad thoughts. In Sunday school they told us bad thoughts come from the Devil. I used to think that was true, but I don't know no more. Perhaps bad thoughts come from other people and the things what they do.

I got some new pictures from the newsagent. They are supposed to be like birthday cards, but I bought them for the pictures they got on them. There is this one picture of this kitten. Its eyes are all funny because there is this butterfly on its nose.

The butterfly is all colours, like red and yellow and green.

The other picture is a bunny rabbit. The bunny rabbit is blue. I know bunny rabbits aren't blue in real life, but this one is blue because that's how it's drawn. It is cute. It's like all smiley and fluffy and nothing wrong with it.

I put the pictures on my bedside table so I can see them when I go to bed and then when I wake up first thing in the morning. Even if I wake up in the night, I'll know they're there, having nice smiles.

I'd like to dream about the kitten and the bunny rabbit. I'd like to dream about Nanna, too. Sometimes I do dream about her, but I can't do it just by thinking. I never been able to do that. Most of my dreams aren't nice, with monsters, and Dracula biting me and swallowing my blood. They are nightmares. They're just dreams, and dreams can't hurt me, but when I have them they hurt and I am frightened. Sometimes I wake up and they're still happening. I don't like them dreams. Dreams should stop in the dark and leave you alone instead of following you.

NO MORE SCHOOL FOR 2 DAYS.

I wish it could be holidays all the time. I can do what I want in the holidays. There is no Billy Pickett and people saying things. I can make up a friend to play with, and we have good games together.

I have written ever such a lot in this book. If I carry on, I'll have to get another one. I think if I go on writing, it will help my school writing.

I don't know about my feelings though. I don't know if it is helping with them. I don't know what helps with feelings. Maybe you just have to wait until they go away by themselves. My feelings are taking a long time to go away. I don't know what to do if they don't.

Maybe I'll dream something nice, to put everything all right.

Five

Saturday morning: what to wear?

After Dad bought Liam a computer for Christmas, Mum dragged Liam off to the January sales in London and hit the hippest clothes shops. She treated it like it was a competition between her and Dad – the one who spent the most money on Liam was the one who cared most about him. Liam had gone along with it, letting Mum do the choosing, hating the way she used her posh voice when she talked to the sales assistants, hating the way she waved her American Express gold card under their noses. Liam ended up with an outfit that made him look like a Star Fleet Academy cadet. He'd only worn the whole thing together once, preferring to wear the bits separately and mix them with other things.

He shouldn't wear anything too new or too flash; he didn't want to out-designer-label anyone. Neutral: faded blue jeans that were starting to fray around the pockets, scuffed trainers, a short-sleeved T-shirt and a navy-blue woollen jacket that was a bit like a scuba diving top, with a big chrome toggle on the zipper.

Liam examined himself in the mirror and saw that he'd do. If he passed himself in the street, he wouldn't look twice.

The rendezvous was the bus stops outside St Mary's churchyard. St Mary's was imposing, its walls chequered with slabs of black flint and grey limestone. There were huge trees in the churchyard. At the foot of one of the trees sat a group of alkies, passing round a bottle in a brown paper bag. The alkies were having an intense discussion about something; they smoothed the air with their hands as though they were shaping lumps of invisible clay.

Across the road from the bus stops stood the mall, a brutal block of concrete wrapped in glaring strips of neon. A flag flew from a pole on the roof. The flag had *St Mary's Shopping Centre* printed on it in fading letters.

To the left of the mall was a side street, occupied by an open air market. Liam watched the crowds in the market, killing time by counting all the people who were wearing something red. He'd arrived fifteen minutes early – early enough to worry. What if he'd got the wrong bus stops? What if Billy didn't show? It could be a practical joke – arrange to meet and then not turn up, so that Liam would know he'd been taken for a wally. Or maybe, and this was difficult for Liam to get his head around, he didn't want Billy to come. He'd got in with Billy because at school Billy was the one everybody was scared of. Outside school, Liam wasn't certain what he thought about Billy; he wasn't even sure that he liked him. Liam had a sudden urge to forget the whole thing and go home. He'd dream up some excuse, give Billy a call later . . .

But it was too late. A bus pulled up at the kerb and Billy tumbled out of it, wearing black jeans and a black bomber jacket. He looked different out of uniform; scrawnier. He smiled as he walked over to Liam, a smug smile, like he was chuffed that Liam was right where he'd been told to be.

Billy said, 'Any sign of Des?'

'No,' said Liam.

Billy rolled his eyes. 'Never on time for anything, that kid. He'll be late for his own funeral.' He pulled a packet of cigarettes from his pocket, flipped back the top and offered it to Liam. 'Want a fag?'

Liam thought quickly: if he refused, he'd look soft, but if he took a cigarette he wouldn't know what to do with it, and it would be obvious that he'd never smoked one before. He was in a no-win situation.

Inspiration galloped to the rescue. 'Not for me, thanks. I tried it once and my dad caught me. He made me smoke the whole packet, one after the other, till I puked. It put me off for life.'

'Yeah? My dad did the same thing to me, and I·loved it.' Billy lit up and sucked down a lungful of smoke, exhaling it through his nose.

'Does your mum know?'

'Yeah. She's OK with it. She was smoking when she was my age.'

'Aren't you afraid you might get cancer?'

Billy shrugged with his mouth. 'If you start worrying about all the things that can kill you, you'll go mental. My uncle choked to death on a chicken bone, but it didn't put me off eating. Loads of people get killed in motorway pile-ups, but there's still plenty of traffic about, isn't there?'

'Good point,' said Liam, not knowing what the point was. 'Where are we going when Des gets here?'

'Check out Virgin, have a look at the new video games, see if we can do a bus number.'

'What's a bus number?' said Liam, wondering if it was like train-spotting.

Billy smiled his smug smile again and said, 'A-a-a-ah!' Des arrived at ten to two. He'd missed the earlier bus because he'd had to take his little sister round to his grandparents' house. Des was wearing a leather jacket, tan chinos and oxblood loafers. He looked about nineteen.

Billy said, 'What's with the get-up? Hoping to pull?'

'My other stuff's in the wash. This is my gospel singer look. Hallelujah, bro! Blessed is de name of de Lawd!'

They did the downstairs of Virgin, taking in CDs and posters. Liam listened carefully as Billy did a rundown of the top thirty albums, so that he'd know what opinion to have. Gangsta was cool, heavy metal was cool as long as it was about satanism; boy bands and guitar bands were naff. *Bella-Bella 14*'s music was naff, but the young women who sang it weren't. Billy stared hot-eyed at a poster of the group. 'Which one d'you fancy, Lee?'

'Tammy,' said Liam. It was a safe bet: Tammy had famously come out of the top of her dress when the group picked up an award at the Brits.

'Yeah, she's horny,' said Billy. 'I like the French-looking one.'

'That's Tray,' said Des. 'I fancy all of 'em. I wouldn't say no to any of 'em.'

The video games were upstairs. Billy browsed through the racks going, 'Rubbish, rubbish, kids' stuff, cool, rubbish. Nothing new. I was hoping they'd have that game in from the States, the one where you shoot-up a high school. You get extra points for the teachers.'

'No chance. Been banned,' said Des. 'Bit sick, really.'

'Sounds like a laugh,' said Billy. 'Hey, be great to do it for real, wouldn't it? Like up on the swimming-pool roof with a kalashnikov at break. Pow! Bye-bye, Boggy Marsh!'

Des said, 'Pow! Bye-bye, Harry!'

Liam thought fast. He needed to come up with a name that Billy would think was funny. 'Pow! Bye-bye, Ella Thickie!'

Billy went into American newsreader-mode. 'It's incredible! They've been pouring bullets into her, but she just keeps on coming!'

Liam got a picture: cartoon Ella Thickie, staring in disbelief as jets of blood pumped out of her wounds. He said, 'She's dead, but she's too dumb to lie down!'

Billy and Des cracked up; it gave Liam a glow.

Inside the mall was a water-feature: a wall of glass stretching from the ceiling to a fern-edged pool. Water ran down the wall in a constant stream, making the glass waver as though it were melting.

Two security guards were leaning against the upper-floor balcony, gazing down at the shoppers below. Their peaked caps and khaki shirts made them look like American cops but with handsets on their hips instead of Magnums.

Billy took the guards in with a flick of his eyes. 'Clock the heavy mob, lads,' he said. 'We'll have to take it steady.'

'Not much doing here, anyway,' said Des. 'We'd be better off round Tesco's.'

'Better off for what?' said Liam.

'Bus number,' Billy said.

The supermarket was out of the guards' field of vision. Billy, Des and Liam stood outside. Billy and Des were watching the customers come and go.

A middle-aged woman came through the automatic doors, carrying bulging plastic bags in both hands.

'How about her?' said Des.

'Nah,' said Billy.

'I reckon I could give her a go,' Des said.

'No way!' said Billy. 'She'd suss you straight off in those clothes.' He stiffened. 'Now her, on the other hand . . .' he said.

Billy's eyes were fixed on an old woman in a brown overcoat and a shapeless beige hat. She was reading the 'Special Offer' notices on the supermarket windows.

Billy said to Liam, 'Watch and learn.' He went over to the old woman and spoke to her. She turned to him, cocked her head as though she hadn't heard him properly. Billy's face was a picture of misery, he seemed to be on the verge of tears.

'What's he doing?' said Liam.

Des said, 'A bus number. He's giving her a sob story about how some kids nicked his wallet, and now he doesn't have the bus-fare home, and it's miles away. He's good at it.'

He was: the old woman took out her purse, rummaged inside and held a clenched hand out to Billy. Billy shook his head. Liam saw his lips move: *No, I couldn't, really.*

The old woman insisted, pressed something into Billy's hand. Billy's expression went from surprised, to embarrassed, to grateful.

Des said, 'Result! Come on, we'll wait for him outside the toy shop. If she sees him with us, she'll twig.'

Billy appeared after two minutes. 'Old bat gave me a couple of quid, didn't she?'

Liam said, 'That must be a lot to a pensioner like her.'

'What's she got to spend money on at her age?' said Billy. 'Had her life, hasn't she? Old people are useless. They ought to bring in euthanasia to get rid of them. Costing us millions, they are.'

Des put on a cracked, shaky voice. 'Ooh, you young people today ain't got no respect for anything!'

Billy said, 'Old people have got it in for us because we're young and they're past it. Anyway, I made that old biddy's day. She got a big kick out of giving someone a helping hand. What could she buy for two quid that'd make her feel that good?'

Liam was uneasy: it wasn't exactly stealing, more a game; it didn't harm anyone, but it still felt wrong.

Billy said, 'If she's stupid enough to give her money away, I'd be stupid not to take it, wouldn't I?'

All around them, signs said: *BUY NOW! TAKE ADVANTAGE OF OUR AMAZING OFFER!! SPEND £££s SAVE ££££££s!!!*

The bus number, in one form or another, was what made the world go around.

Billy selected his next victims at the open air market, an elderly couple buying cheese from a stall.

Billy said, 'They've got to be up for it, haven't they? Should be good for at least a fiver. Take 'em, Lee.'

'Me?' said Liam. 'I couldn't. I'd blow it.'

'Piece of duff! Just give it loads of –' Billy made his eyes sad, pushed his voice up into a snivelling whine. 'Please, sir, I don't know what to do. Some boys took my wallet, and now I can't get home.' His voice went back to normal. 'They'll cough up.'

Liam fought down panic. 'I can't.'

Billy said, 'What's the matter? Haven't you got the bottle for it?'

It was crunch time. Either Liam was on Billy's side or he wasn't, and if he wasn't, Billy was going to make

school hell. He'd call him 'Lily', or something like that –
Liam knew he would.

Des said, 'Come on, come on, they're leaving! Go for
it, Lee!'

Liam stumbled forwards, empty-stomached, empty-
legged. The side of his mouth was twitching. It was
dream-like, awful: the old woman had a hairy wart on
her left cheek; the old man's nose was caught in a net of
broken veins.

Liam said, 'Oh, er, excuse me! Sorry to bother you.'

The old man had milky-blue eyes. 'What's the matter,
son?'

Liam looked at the ground. 'I think I'm lost. Can you
tell me where the station is, please?'

'Bus or train?'

Liam couldn't make sense of the words; it was like
the old man was talking a foreign language. 'I beg your
pardon?' he said.

'Bus station or train station?'

'Train station.'

'Easy. Go through the churchyard, take your first left,
next right, left by the Nationwide office and carry straight
on. Take you about five minutes.'

'Thank you,' said Liam. He walked away, his face
burning. Billy and Des had vanished. Liam didn't know
where to go, but he had to get out of the crowds. He

pushed his way through to open space and gulped air.

Billy and Des materialised either side of him. Des was giggling so hard that he couldn't speak. Billy's eyes were cruel with laughter. 'You should have seen your face! You looked like you were going to mess your pants!'

'They wouldn't give me anything. The old man told me that he'd fetch the police if I didn't push off.'

Billy said, 'You were –' and he gawped like a fish on a slab.

Des caught hold of a lamp post to keep himself upright.

'I was useless. I'm just not in your class, Billy,' said Liam.

'Never mind,' said Billy. 'It was worth it to see your face.'

Liam stuck a finger into the side of his chin and went, 'Doh!' like Homer Simpson.

'I'm starving. Let's go to McDonald's,' said Billy.

Liam's insides were squirming like he had a gut full of worms.

Six

Sunday was a nothing day: closed shops, empty streets; the air was shrill with the snarling of lawnmowers.

Liam spent the morning finishing off his art home-work and thinking about Saturday afternoon. He'd bottled out of asking the old couple for a hand-out, but he'd got away with it by clowning. Billy hadn't asked him to try it on with anyone else, just laughed until Liam's sense of shame had faded into the togetherness of a private joke. Liam didn't feel as if he stuck out so much now that he had Billy and Des – and Bing too, probably, but Bing wasn't so easy to know; he didn't have words the way that Billy and Des did.

The afternoon in town had helped Liam to get his place in the group clear. He was the klutz, the one who got everything wrong. The trick was to be wrong in a way that didn't make him look too stupid, and Liam had learned that the way to do that was to dress his failures up in a way that made Billy look good.

The art homework was 'Something Important from the Past'. Liam painted a remote controlled car: black tinted windows, gleaming chrome, red, go-faster lightning-bolts on the side. He'd chosen it because it was easy to paint. In fact, the most important toy from his childhood was a cheap, plastic glider, but he didn't paint it, because why it was important wouldn't fit into a picture. He remembered launching the glider from the top of the slide in the adventure playground near his old house, and the excitement of watching the little plane swoop and drift. No two flights were ever the same, but the excitement always was. The glider made him uncomplicatedly happy, and it was one of the few toys that he'd bought himself. The rest of his toys were presents from Mum and Dad, toys they thought a boy should have, like a train set and a mountain bike.

Toys had stopped in year six. One of Dad's most repeated warnings had been, 'Don't be in such a hurry to grow up,' but then he started buying Liam clothes, deodorant and pen sets as birthday and Christmas presents. Dad had described the PC as 'an educational tool' which made it sound more like an investment in Liam's future than a gift. Liam wondered what Dad would say if he knew that the computer was mostly used for playing games – then wondered why he was wondering what Dad would say about anything.

What Dad thought didn't matter that much any more.

Mum gave Liam a second watch-for-danger sign after lunch. The phone rang and Mum went to answer it. Liam heard her say, 'Oh, hello, Paul!' and she was as breathy as a teenager in a soap opera, cooing and trilling into the mouthpiece. Liam glanced into the hall and saw that Mum had the flex of the phone wrapped around the fingers of her left hand. Her right knee was bent and she was moving her foot so that her shoe slipped on and off her heel – bop, bop, bop.

Liam frowned. Mum was looking for someone to happen to. She wanted to prove to Dad that if he could find someone new, so could she. Liam considered the prospect of a stepfather and went cold: there were enough strangers in the house as it was.

Liam carried the dirty lunch plates to the kitchen and slotted them into the dishwasher. He heard the phone peep as Mum replaced the receiver. She came through to the kitchen, with a big smile on her face.

'You look pleased,' said Liam.

'That was Paul. He said I did a good job yesterday. He's promised to take me out to dinner one evening next week to say thank you properly. Isn't that nice of him?'

'Mm. Is he married?'

'What's that got to do with anything?'

'Nothing.'

'Paul's my boss. Our relationship is strictly professional. I don't know anything about his private life and I don't want to know. That's his business.'

'Right.'

'I can do without you trying to match-make, thanks very much. I don't need another involvement at the moment. I'm perfectly content as I am.'

'Good.'

It was neat the way Mum had turned things round on him.

The phone rang again at half-four. Mum was upstairs, working in the spare bedroom that she'd converted into an office. Liam was in the lounge, watching a made-for-TV movie about a marriage break-up. He went to the phone, shouting up the stairs, 'I'll get it!' He picked up the receiver and said, 'Hello?'

It was Dad. 'Liam! How you doing?'

Liam's insides went to slush. 'All right. D'you want me to fetch Mum?'

'No, don't bother her. It was you I wanted to talk to, actually. How are you getting on? What's the new school like?'

'All right.'

'Settled in?'

'Yeah.'

'How does it compare with your other school?'

'About the same.'

A moment's silence, then Dad said, 'Look, Liam, I'm sorry we haven't seen much of each other. It's not that I didn't want to, it's just, you know, I've been busy at work, and getting the new place into shape, and –'

'No worries.'

'I promise I'll get my act together so you can come for a weekend next month, OK?'

Liam didn't want to spend a weekend with Dad. 'Sure.'

'I haven't been fair to your mum, either. I mean, I've let her shoulder all the responsibility for you.'

He meant that Liam was something to dump, and he felt guilty about not giving Mum a break.

'So, how are the teachers at the new school? Strict, I hope.'

'They're all right.'

'Made any friends?'

'A couple.'

'Good. Got a girlfriend yet?'

'Da-ad!'

'Time you did. I was on my second girlfriend when I was your age.'

Liam wondered how many girlfriends that made now – had Dad kept score? 'There's no rush.'

'Don't you believe it.'

There came an awkwardness. Dad breathed hard and it made a noise like the sound of the sea in a shell. 'What I really rang for was to ask you how you'd feel about having a baby brother or sister.'

'What?'

'Mia's going to have a baby. We got the results of the test back last week.'

'Oh?'

'Yeah. We're both delighted, of course.'

'Congratulations.'

'I wanted to let you know myself, make sure you're OK with it.'

Like if Liam wasn't, it would make a difference?

'I wanted you to know that . . . the new baby and everything . . . well, you're still my son, yeah? I'm still your dad. Nothing's going to change that. You're just as important to me as you've always been.'

And how important was that? Important enough to ring up, but not important enough to stick around for.

'I know that. You don't have to –'

'Yes, I do.'

Liam was floundering: any minute now Dad was going to tell him he loved him, and Liam didn't want to hear it.

Dad said, 'Er, look, I was wondering if you wouldn't mind telling your mum about Mia. I think she'd take it better from you than she would from me.'

'Sure.'

'Cheers.'

'Dad, I've got to go. I've got some mates over. We're in the middle of this game of –'

'Oh, right,' said Dad, sounding relieved. 'Better let you get back to it then. I'll be in touch about that weekend, so see you in a few weeks, yeah?'

'Yeah. Bye.' Liam put the phone back in its cradle while a memory rushed at him.

Dad had told him about what was happening, in the dining-room of the old house. Dad had sat with his hands one on top of the other on the table and said, 'Your mum and I, we didn't know that things would go wrong. Things happen. People change. Sometimes they don't realise they've changed until it's too late to go back. No one meant to hurt anybody.'

But no one had done anything to stop the hurt from happening.

Mum appeared at the top of the stairs. 'Who was that?'

'Dad.'

Mum's voice dropped ten degrees. 'What did he want?'

'Not a lot. Mia's pregnant.'

Mum's face went hard. 'Bet that was her idea.'

Adults sucked: they pretended to care, pretended to know everything; but they only cared about themselves and they knew zilch. Billy was right about older people having it in for the young – why else would parents go to so much trouble to make their children's lives a misery?

Ella's Diary

Dad is worried about work. He came home on Friday and said he reckoned the council are going to lay people off, and he's worried they might lay him off. He's worried he's too old to get another job. He says when you are gone forty you are past it.

We got to cut down in case. We got to go to Betta Shoppa instead of Asda. I don't like Betta Shoppa stuff. Their Rice Crispies is all cardboardy and the bread is so thin it makes hard toast.

We seen Mrs Bates in Betta Shoppa. We haven't met her for ages. She looks like a little old woman now, with all white hair, and her face got all lines on it and stuff. She said, 'Ooh, Ella! Haven't you grown! You are all grown up!'

I went red. I thought she meant I was fat. I can't help it. The doctor says it is glandular. Like I got all things inside of me what make me fat. Nanna used to say, Who wants to be thin and miserable? It's better to be fat and jolly. But I'm not jolly.

I wish I was thin like them models in the pictures on posters. I wish I didn't have glandular.

In the afternoon we went round Aunty May's. I played with the baby. They are going to call her Rosy, after Nanna. I think Nanna would of liked that. She would of liked Rosy, because Rosy is all rosy, with pink cheeks. She got a laugh like a stream going over pebbles. When she chuckles, it makes me chuckle. One day I'll have a chuckly baby, and I will love her to bits.

I had a monster dream Saturday night. In the dream, I wanted to go to the toilet but I couldn't because there was this huge spider on the wall and I didn't want it to land on me. I was dying to go but I couldn't. It was funny, because I am not frightened of spiders when I am awake, but I was frightened in the dream.

I was supposed to go to Sunday school on Sunday, but I didn't. I told Mum and Dad I went, but I never. I went to Nanna. I haven't been for a while. There was weeds on her grave, so I pulled them up. I sat down in the sunshine and talked to Nanna in my head. She said, 'You're a good girl, Ella. You're a good, sweet girl. You got a loving nature. You are kind and gentle. Don't you mind what people say about you. Sticks and stones may break your bones, but names will never hurt you.'

It was quiet with Nanna in the graveyard. It would be nice to have a talk with someone like Nanna, but there is no one else like her. She was the only Nanna there was.

School tomorrow. I can feel school inside. It's like a big crab with big pincers, all sticking in me. It squeezes the pincers tight, tight, tight.

IF THAT BILLY PICKETT STARTS ON AT ME AGAIN, I'LL KILL HIM. I'LL CHOKE HIM TILL HIS FACE GOES BLACK AND HIS TONGUE STICKS OUT.

In Sunday school once, they read out this bit in the Bible where Jesus says we got to love our enemies, but I don't love Billy Pickett. I hate him. Why is he alive when nice people like Nanna are dead?

Sometimes I think that God forgot about the world after he made it. He told the people they should be nice to everyone, and then he went away somewhere to do something else, and he forgot about us and let the Devil take over.

I wish God would come back and make it all right. I wish he would make people stop saying things about me. I wish he would take the crab from inside me so I would like going to school.

I don't know if I can take much more. I try to be strong, but it isn't easy.

Seven

The last thing Billy had said to Liam on Saturday afternoon was, 'Meet me down the end of my street, Monday morning, eight-thirty. We'll walk to school together, yeah?'

Liam had taken it as an order, not a suggestion. He was at the corner of Dryden Crescent at eight twenty-five. Eight-thirty arrived and Billy didn't. Over the next five minutes Liam got twitchy, shuffling his feet like a little boy bursting for a pee. Time was getting critical: the bell for registration went at five to nine. If Liam didn't go soon, he wouldn't make it. He was just about to give up when he saw Billy. Liam put on a reflex grin, but as Billy got closer the grin shrank into neutral.

Billy had dark light coming off him. His mouth looked like he'd been sucking something bitter.

'I thought I might have missed you.'

Billy didn't say anything. He walked straight past Liam, as if Liam were a tree. Liam hurried to catch up, fell into step and said, 'We'll be late if we don't get a move on.'

'So?' Billy's voice was sulky; he was in a strop.

'Everything all right?'

'Yeah. Any reason it shouldn't be?'

'No. Only you look . . .'

Billy turned his head, glared. 'I look what?'

'Nothing.'

'Leave it. Just leave it, OK?' Billy was seething.

Liam held up his hands, palms turned outwards. 'Sorry.' He didn't know what he was apologising for.

Billy was quiet all the way to school.

Liam didn't try any jokes; he was walking next to an unexploded bomb, and it was ticking.

The registration bell sounded when they were twenty metres from the school gate.

'Shall we run?' asked Liam.

'You can, if you want. I'm not going to. Stuff it.'

'We'll get a late mark.'

Three late marks meant an automatic detention.

'Big deal. Go ahead, if you're worried.'

It was a test of loyalty; Liam stayed with Billy.

As it happened they didn't get a late mark, because the staff meeting over-ran. They joined Bing and Des in the Eight Luke West queue. Bing and Des did just what Liam had done: they smiled when they first saw Billy, then stopped smiling when he ignored their greetings. They looked question marks at Liam; Liam shrugged.

Mr Cooper turned up at five past nine. 'Apologies for lateness, Eight LW,' he said. 'I know how much you've been pining for a glimpse of my ruggedly handsome features. In you go. Try not to trample anybody.' He looked at Billy. 'Lighten up, William. It may never happen.'

'It already hasn't happened.'

Mr Cooper chose not to comment on what Billy said, or the fact that he hadn't said 'sir'.

Billy detonated in lesson two, maths with Mr Marsh. Mr Marsh handed back the homework he'd collected on Friday, giving a brief comment to each pupil. Liam got, 'Well done.' Bing got, 'Keep taking the tablets, Simon.' When all the books had been given out, Mr Marsh perched on the edge of his desk, his left hand in his trouser pocket; casual and tense. He said, 'Where was yours, Billy?'

Billy said, 'What?'

'Your book. Where was your book?'

'Forgot to hand it in, didn't I?'

The air stiffened like beaten egg-white.

'And why was that?' Mr Marsh said evenly. He was letting Billy wind himself in.

'I couldn't do the homework. It was too hard.'

'The other members of the class didn't seem to think so.'

'I didn't get it.'

Mr Marsh pursed his lips and nodded slowly. 'If you had trouble with the work, why didn't you mention it when I took the books in on Friday?'

Billy said, 'Told you, didn't I? I forgot.'

Two pinpoint gleams of annoyance showed in Mr Marsh's eyes. 'If I were an uncharitable person, Billy, I'd be inclined not to believe you.'

'Believe what you like.'

The room went still. It was the Billy and Mr Marsh Show; everybody else was the audience. It reminded Liam of the way the old house had felt when Mum and Dad were having a row.

Mr Marsh said, 'I don't much care for your attitude, young man. Sit up straight when you talk to me. Stop slouching!'

Billy blinked as lazily as a lizard in the sun. 'Gonna make me?'

Mr Marsh smiled, showing his teeth. 'You're full of yourself, Billy. You really think you're it, don't you? Well, from where I'm standing, you look like an insolent little brat.'

'And you look like a fat git . . . *sir.*'

Mr Marsh turned into Robot Teacher; his voice was toneless. 'I've wasted quite enough of the class's time on you, Pickett. Go to Mrs Lynn's office.'

Billy didn't move.

'Now!' said Mr Marsh.

Billy stood with a weary sigh, the legs of his chair squealing against the floor tiles. He thrust his books into his bag and swaggered out: maximum charisma points.

Mr Marsh carried on with the lesson as though nothing had happened.

There were rumours at break time: Billy had walked out of school; Mrs Lynn had sent for his mother; Billy had been expelled. Most people seemed to be enjoying it, like Billy Pickett had finally got his comeuppance and they were glad.

Des, Bing and Liam talked it up.

Des said, 'Billy was dead cool. He certainly told Boggy Marsh where to get off, didn't he?'

'Boggy was asking for it,' said Bing.

'Billy's a legend,' said Liam. He didn't understand: Billy had forced a showdown with one of the strictest teachers in the school; he must have known that he didn't have a hope of getting away with it; it had been a kind of suicide. 'What'll they do to Billy?'

'Nothing he can't handle,' Des said confidently.

Bing said, 'I thought Billy was going to stick one on Boggy. Be tops if he had, wouldn't it?'

And, according to the rumours circulating by lunchtime, Billy had. Some people said he'd punched Mr Marsh out, others had it the other way round – Mr Marsh had taken a swing at Billy and was going to have to resign because of it.

Mr Cooper revealed the truth at afternoon registration. He said, 'There's been a lot of wild speculation about what happened in maths this morning, and the head has asked the staff to make an announcement to put an end to it. You know what took place, because you were there, so I won't bother to go into that. Perhaps some of you think it was big for Billy to be disrespectful to a teacher. I don't. I find it sad. A large school like ours depends on mutual respect between pupils and teachers. I don't know what made Billy forget that, but the head has excluded him from lessons for a week to reflect on what he's done. If he doesn't apologise to Mr Marsh at the end of that time, he'll be excluded for another week, and if he still doesn't apologise, he'll be excluded permanently. Exclusion is a very serious matter. It's the school's way of saying that if you can't accept our rules, we don't want you in our community.'

Liam blushed like *he* was the one who'd been excluded.

Mr Cooper said, 'Off you go, Eight LW.'

The class filed out. When Liam got to the front, Mr Cooper said, 'Hang on, Liam. I'd like a word.'

Cold scalp, thumping heart; what now?

Mr Cooper waited until the last person had left, then closed the door and said, 'You strike me as a decent kid, Liam. The reports from your last school say you were a model pupil. What are you playing at?'

'Sir?'

'Don't come it, Liam,' said Mr Cooper. 'You know exactly what I'm talking about. You don't belong with Billy Pickett and his mates. They're not your sort.'

Like, what would Mr Cooper know about it? He was just playing Wise Dad because it was in his job description; he didn't actually care.

'If you go round with Billy Pickett, you'll end up tarred with the same brush. You'll get a bad reputation, and reputation is a funny thing. You can't see it and you can't touch it, but you can't lose it, either. Mud sticks at Oxfield Comp.'

'Yes, sir.'

'You're worth more than that. You're going to carry what you achieve at this school with you for the rest of your life. Wise up, Liam. Stop playing silly whatsits with your future.'

Liam wasn't sure if he should say yes or no to this, so he settled for, 'Sir.'

'Be more careful about your choice of friends,' said Mr Cooper.

Part of Liam knew that Mr Cooper was right; another part resented him for sticking his nose in. Liam had no control over where he lived, what school he went to, or what he learned when he got there – but his friends were his. He'd come to Oxfield Comp with no one, and they'd taken him in. Mr Cooper was out of order: it wasn't for a teacher to decide whom Liam should or shouldn't hang out with.

'Yes, sir.'

Mr Cooper's eyes said that he knew he'd wasted his time.

At the end of school, Liam started the walk home with Bing. It was the first time they'd been on their own together. All Liam knew about Bing was what not to talk about – Bing's black eye – so getting a conversation going was like trying to start a car with a dead battery.

'Good weekend?' Liam asked.

'Boring.'

They went two more paces.

Liam said, 'Got a computer?'

'Can't afford one.'

Another slammed door.

Liam said, 'So . . . what football team d'you support?'

'Chelsea and Man United,' said Bing. It was a Billy-echo; Bing even sounded like Billy when he said it.

Liam said, 'Hey, did you see that film on telly yesterday afternoon? It was about –'

'You talk funny, don't you?' said Bing.

'Do I?'

'Yeah. Your voice is a bit, like, la-de-da, innit? You don't talk like you come from round here.'

Liam made an instant adjustment to his accent. 'Put it on, don't I? You can get away with murder if you talk proper.'

'That right?' said Bing. He saw straight through Liam, but it didn't matter, because he was Bing. In Billy's group, Bing was below Liam.

Billy was waiting outside Liam's house, wearing his Saturday clothes, a cigarette dangling from the corner of his mouth.

Liam knew he was privileged to be the one Billy had come to, but he wasn't keen on the neighbours seeing them together: if someone told Mum that Liam was mixing with smokers, she'd freak.

Liam held his hand like there was a microphone in it, and said, 'Please put your hands together to welcome my very special guest star, Mr Exclusion!'

'You heard, then? Brilliant, eh? I give Boggy a mouthful, and they give me a week's holiday.'

'Yeah,' said Liam. 'Cool.'

'I couldn't hack it. When Boggy started going on at me, giving it sarky, I lost it.'

'Are you going to apologise to him at the end of the week?'

Billy laughed. 'Might do. Don't have to mean it though, do I?'

'Mr Cooper told us you'd be expelled if you didn't.'

Billy took a last drag of his cigarette and flicked it away; it landed on the road in a shower of sparks. 'Well, we can't have that, can we? Wouldn't be any fun without me around.'

'Too right,' said Liam.

Billy focused his eyes somewhere in the middle distance and said, 'It's my kid sister's birthday today. She got a card from my dad, first thing this morning. Never sends me a card, does he? Like, I don't matter to him.'

'My dad's the same. Always forgets my birthday.'

Not true: Dad wouldn't dare forget; it would put Mum one up.

'Dads, eh? Can't wait to get shot of you,' Billy said.

'Some bimbo came on to my dad and he was off like a rat up a drain. Want to come in for a bit?'

Billy considered it. 'Yeah, all right.'

Liam hoped he wouldn't stay long. He was afraid that when Billy saw him on his home ground, Billy would suss him out, twig that he was pretending to be someone he wasn't. When Mr Cooper had said that Billy wasn't Liam's sort, Liam had resented it because he thought that Mr Cooper had been interfering; now he wondered if Mr Cooper had been trying to warn him.

Ella's Diary

THIS IS MY BEST DAY EVER.

BILLY PICKETT GOT CHUCKED OUT OF SCHOOL. HE'S NOT COMING BACK NO MORE. SERVES HIM RIGHT.

He got into this fight with Mr Marsh. He lost his temper and hit him. That is the worst thing what you can do to a teacher. Billy Pickett has gone too far this time. He has had it.

I feel like having a party. I feel like pop-bubbles inside. I feel like all the clouds have gone and the sun is shining. I won't have to take no more from Billy Pickett.

I'm getting used to this diary. It's a friend to me. I can put stuff in it that I couldn't say to no one, but maybe now Billy Pickett is gone I won't have nothing to put. I put my dark times in the diary, all the things I shouldn't really be thinking. It's better than keeping them locked up. When you're afraid of something, it's better to take it out and have a good look at it, 'cos feelings make things seem bigger than what they really are.

Now I'm all bright inside.

Mr Clark says I am coming along. He says there is nothing wrong with what I got to say, like when I'm talking I'm all right, but when I put it down my spelling is mixed-up. He says a lot of famous people got dys. I didn't know that. I didn't know you could have dys and be famous. I don't know why we got to have spelling and letters in the right order. Mr Clark says English is one of the hardest languages to spell. He is dead right there. English is stupid when it comes to spelling.

In school they put up this picture of a baby seal. The baby seal is white and furry, and it's got big eyes, and it makes you want to pick it up and cuddle it. But these men come with like bats and they hit the baby seals over the head. I don't know how they can do that. I couldn't. I couldn't be cruel to no little baby seal. They must have something wrong with them, like in their minds. It's worse than having dys, 'cos in dys you get like your letters mixed-up, but them men with bats got their feelings mixed-up.

When I am grown up, I am going to save the baby seals. I am going to go where they are and stop the men with bats from killing them. I will make like a home for them where they can live and be safe. I would give them milk to drink, and fish when they got older. Then I would let them go. Maybe they would come back with their own babies to show me because I was kind to them. Nanna used to say that what you do, kind or cruel, comes back to you in the end. I only want kind to come back to me.

That's why I'm not cruel, only in my thoughts to cruel people.

Tonight I'm going to try and dream about baby seals in a warm place where it is safe, and they'll look at me with their big eyes, and I'll be safe and warm too.

Eight

With Billy out of the way, Eight Luke West became a different form. They relaxed, told one another jokes. Teachers got a better response because people dared to put up their hands and answer questions when Billy wasn't there to jeer at them for being clever.

There were changes in Billy's group, too. Des sat with Imran Mullik and Bing paired up with Chris Michael. This left Liam on his own, but not feeling isolated. Eight Luke West tolerated him.

Last lesson on Tuesday was music. After the final bell went, Liam hung round the foyer of the Elgar Block to avoid having to walk home with Bing. Liam pretended to read the notices on the boards. He wouldn't have to wait long; five minutes should do it.

The door of one of the practice rooms was open and the sound of someone playing the guitar drifted out of it.

Liam could only hear snatches because of the home-time stampede, but as the building emptied, the guitar became more audible. Notes rippled, swam into patterns. A voice hummed a simple, sad tune. The tune pulled Liam towards the open door, made him look inside.

A boy sat hunched over a Spanish guitar, the fingers of his left hand splayed across the fretboard, the fingers of his right hand moving rhythmically as he plucked at the strings. Liam couldn't see the boy's face, just a mass of black hair and a pointed chin pressed against the curve of the guitar's shoulder.

All at once it struck Liam that he was intruding. He made to go, and the movement broke the boy's concentration. He stopped playing, raised his head and pinned Liam with his clear grey eyes.

The boy said, 'You want something?'

'No,' said Liam. 'Sorry. I was just listening. You're pretty good.'

'Not as good as I ought to be. I've been learning since I was eight, but I can't stick the music they give me to play. I'd rather do rock, you know? Like the early *Oasis* stuff – when they were still cool.' He strummed the opening chords of *Some Might Say*. It didn't sound right on a Spanish guitar.

'Was that an *Oasis* song you were playing before?'

'Nah!' The boy jiggled his shoulders. 'That's something I wrote. Am writing. Trying to write. The tune's OK but I'm having trouble with the lyrics.'

'How far have you got?' said Liam. He was inside the room now. He'd stepped through the doorway without realising.

The boy's eyes went wary. 'You're the new kid in Eight Luke West, right?'

'Right.'

'I've seen you around with Billy Pickett. One of his mates, are you?'

The tone of the boy's voice strongly suggested that this wasn't a good thing to be.

'I wouldn't call us mates exactly, but I know Billy, yeah. Do you?'

'Everybody knows Billy Pickett. He calls me Toilet because my name's Tollit. What a guy, huh?'

Liam said, 'I'm Liam Noakes,' and to his horror, his hand stuck itself out. He couldn't believe that he was doing something so nerdy.

The boy hesitated for a second, then clasped Liam's hand and shook it. 'Ben Tollit. I'm in Eight John North.'

'So, Ben, what about this song? Are you going to play it to me, or what?'

'Got a hankie on you?'

'Huh?'

'To stuff in your mouth so you won't laugh out loud when you hear me sing.'

'I won't laugh.'

Ben waggled his eyebrows. 'You haven't heard the song yet.'

Something about the way he said it made Liam like him, and he smiled. It was his first genuine smile since arriving at Oxfield Comp. 'That bad?'

'On a badness scale of one to ten, it's fifteen.' Ben cleared his throat, chopped out a few chords to check that the strings were still in tune and started singing. His voice was smoky, attractively ragged round the edges; he sang with a startlingly American accent.

> *Why do I*
> *Just sit and cry*
> *When all you do*
> *Is make me blue?*
> *Da-da-da-da*
> *Da-dee-da-da*

He stopped. 'Seriously naff, right?'

'A bit,' said Liam, then worried that he might have trodden too heavily on Ben's toes. 'I mean, it's got potential. Is it about someone?'

'No. It's just words that fit. Sort of.'

'You've got too many notes, or not enough words, or something. Play the first bit again.'

Ben played, and a line came bubbling up from nowhere into Liam's mind. 'Every promise you left broken,' he said.

Ben sang the line and it went with the tune perfectly. 'Hey, Word Boy! That was a bit on the awesome side.'

'I used to be good at writing poetry. I wrote a lot in the juniors, but then I gave up.'

'Why?'

Liam gave a one-shouldered shrug. 'Oh, you know.'

'Because poetry's poofy and can seriously damage your cred?'

'Something like that.'

'Try telling people you want to be a songwriter. They look at you like you've just beamed-in from Weirdo Central. You want to go for line two?'

'Sure, why not?' said Liam. He scrabbled in his bag for his pencil case and rough book. 'Fire away.'

The words came quickly, as though they were using Liam to get themselves down on paper.

Every promise you left broken
Every empty lie
All the things you left unspoken
All the tears I cried
All the times I spoke to you

Not a single word got through
And now you want to make things clear
It's me who doesn't want to hear
Your smile is false your words are cracked
You lost me and there's no way back

Ben sang it through and said, 'H-e-e-y! What say we form a partnership, make millions, win all the awards going and have attractive, hysterical girls fling themselves at us wherever we go?'

Liam put on a dumb voice and said, 'Yeah, all right. Nothing else to do, is there?'

Ben did radio DJ and said, 'Tell me, Liam, what inspired you to write the lyrics of your internationally best-selling poptastic hit?'

'Dunno, mate!' said Liam, but he did: the song was about his parents.

They left it loose, like: must get together and do it again some time; nothing definite. Liam walked home feeling that he'd made a bond. Ben was interesting and funny, a lot like the friends Liam had left behind at his old school. Liam had forgotten how, with some people, you didn't have to try too hard; you just met them and got on with them, straight off.

When he got in, Liam saw the red light of the answerphone winking. He pressed the 'Play' button, muttering, 'What's the excuse tonight, Mum?'

Billy's voice came out of the machine: 'Give us a ring.'

That was it: no please, no thank you, no frills; just, I yank the string, you jump.

Liam prickled with resentment. He didn't need Billy Pickett right now, he didn't want to phone him. Then it occurred to him that if he didn't, Billy might call round. That was a definite no-no. The previous evening, Billy had stayed for an hour, making smart-alec comments about the furniture and decorations, stinking the place out with cigarette smoke. When he'd gone, Liam had flushed the dog-ends down the loo and sprayed half a can of air freshener around to kill the smell.

He punched in Billy's number, heard the phone ring the other end, the clatter of the receiver being lifted.

'Yeah?'

'Hi, it's Lee.'

'Took your time, didn't you?'

'Only just got in. Got kept back after school. Music teacher told me off for chewing in class.'

Billy sucked in a breath. 'My, my, you have been a naughty boy, haven't you?'

'Why did you want me to ring you?'

'For a natter, what d'you think? What's been happening?'

'The usual.'

'What they been saying about me?'

Billy wanted praise, wanted to know that the whole school revolved around him; but no one had mentioned him – they'd been too busy enjoying his not being there.

'Oh, like The-Kid-Who-Stood-Up-To-Boggy stuff. We got a lecture on respect for teachers. Don't you dare act like that wicked Billy Pickett.'

'You doing anything tonight?'

Liam said, 'E-e-er . . .'

'Thought we could get together, go for a stroll, have a laugh.'

'Bummer! Can't. We've got visitors. My uncle and aunt are coming for dinner.'

'Can't you get out of it?'

'No chance. Mum says I've got to be there.'

'Pity. I've been thinking. I've come up with a real cracker.'

'Yeah?'

'Tell you about it when I see you. Cheers.' Billy hung up.

Liam nursed the phone, frowning. He was beginning to think he might have made the wrong decision. The half hour with Ben had been more fun than all the time with Billy put together, because sharing was better than sneaking around in someone's shadow. He'd wanted in with Billy and made it, but he hadn't checked where the exit was.

Mum came in late, carrying a bulging briefcase under her arm. 'So-rry!' she said. 'New set of figures arrived just as I was about to leave. I've got to work through them for tomorrow. Shall I phone for a pizza? We could have Chinese if you'd rather, or a curry. Which d'you fancy?'

'Curry,' said Liam. 'Mum, what do you do if you've made friends with someone and you're not sure you want to be friends with them any more?'

The briefcase slipped; Mum steadied it with her right hand. 'Why, have you had an argument with someone?'

'Not exactly.'

'Don't let it worry you. It'll blow over. These things always do. If the friendship is genuine, it'll last. Pop the kettle on for me, will you, darling? I'm gasping for a cup of tea. I must take my briefcase upstairs before I drop it.'

'Right,' said Liam. He went through to the kitchen and filled the kettle. He didn't know why he'd bothered to ask for Mum's advice because it was always the same: put a paper bag over your head, and all your troubles will disappear.

Ella's Diary

I found out that nice boy's name. It is Liam. I know because I heard another boy say.

I was going home from school, and I was going past Elgar Block, and I heard someone singing, and I stopped to listen 'cos it was a nice song. It was like nice and sad at the same time. And I seen that nice boy who goes round with Billy Pickett. It wasn't him singing, it was this other boy I don't know. I seen him before but I don't know his name. I heard him say the nice boy's name. It is Liam.'

It would be nice to be a singer, but I'm no good at singing. Dad says I got a voice like a foghorn. I used to think a foghorn was like this trumpet made of fog, but now I know it is a thing what they use to tell ships when there is fog, so they don't bump into nothing. It's funny the things you get in your mind when you're little.

I helped Mum to get dinner ready. I cut up potatoes, carrots and onions. The onions made me cry. Mum says the way to a man's heart is through his stomach. Like you got to be good at housework if you want a happy marriage. Dad doesn't do nothing round the house. He says it's women's work. I don't know about that. I think it should be share and share alike. It's love what really matters. You got everything when someone loves you.

I got a big secret. I wouldn't tell no one but this diary. The secret is I am in love with Billy off of Neighbours. He is lovely. When I see him on telly I go all funny. If I see a picture of him I am going to put it on my wall, or maybe I'll get a special book and put it in there, and put PRIVATE on the front so no one can't look at it but me. Liam looks a bit like Billy, but not like you want to put his picture in a book. He got a face that makes you want to talk to it. But if I tried to talk to him, I wouldn't know what to say. I'd go all stupid and he'd be embarrassed.

Billy Pickett is still there. He's not in school but he is, kind of thing, 'cos I can feel him. It is like even when he's not around I can feel his eyes, all crawly like slug slime. I thought he wasn't coming back to school no more, but in assembly Mrs Lynn said he'd be back after a week. I wish he wasn't coming back. Maybe when he comes back I'll call him names, like – PICKETT, LICK IT, ROLL IT UP AND FLICK IT.

But if I call him names it would like make me as bad as what he is, and I don't want to be bad. I don't want to be like him. Nanna said two wrongs don't make a right, but some people don't know what's right and what's wrong, or they make out like they don't. Some people say it's like how you're brung up. Like it's your parents not learning you properly. But I think some people are born with bad inside them, and it comes out no matter what their parents do.

If I had a magic lamp, I would rub it and wish that all the bad in people would go away. But I don't think there's no such thing as no magic lamp. That's just fairy tales. There's just good and bad, and there's nothing no one can do about it.

I am tired. I am going asleep now. Night-night, diary. It was nice to talk to you.

Nine

Walking to school on Wednesday morning, Liam took a look at himself and didn't like it much. He was turning into a poser. He wasn't a Lad, like Billy; he was just trying it on, playing dressing-up with his personality, seeing what it felt like to be in with the Bad Boys.

He'd turned into a liar, too. It had started with his parents when everything fell apart. He'd been like: *Yes, Dad. Yes, I understand. I know you can't help your feelings for Mia. I know it wouldn't be right for you to stay with Mum anymore. I know it doesn't mean that you don't care about me. And: Yes, Mum. I understand how angry and jealous you feel. I know how much it hurts that Dad carried on behind your back. Yes, we have to move, make a new start, put the past behind us, look forward to the future.*

Lie after lie after lie: he hadn't understood a thing. He'd agreed with Mum and Dad because he wanted them to stop talking to him about themselves and their feelings, revealing all the stuff that made him squirmy.

They'd been everything once; they'd been all-powerful. Curled up on Dad's lap, surrounded by his warmth and bigness, had been the safest place in the world. When Liam did something that made Mum laugh, it was like turning on a fountain inside. If he did something wrong, their sharp words cut him, their frowns darkened the sky.

Then it had come to pieces. He'd known for a long time that his parents weren't perfect, but he'd never guessed the depth of their imperfection. They were as insecure and confused as he was: worse than he was, because they were insecure and confused about things he didn't really know about. Falling in love – soppy stuff that had made him turn away from the TV and go, '*Yeuk!*' every time people in a film started slobbering over each other – transformed his parents into bleating morons. And what for? Love didn't last: it shifted, changed shape, threw tantrums and evaporated. Mum and Dad had told him too much about it. Liam didn't trust love and he didn't trust them: he couldn't, he had to survive.

So Liam had tried trusting himself. He thought he was less complicated than his parents, with their obsession about who cared most for whom.

Wrong. He turned out to be as unreliable as they

were; he didn't know what he really wanted, any more than they did. Liam had assumed that as he got older things would start to make sense, that there'd come a time when he'd know what he was doing and take charge of his life. Now he had a suspicion that there were no such things as adults – just big, sad children.

The downside to Billy being away was lunch-time. Liam hated eating alone in public, and eating didn't get much more public than lunch at Oxfield Comp. The main hall converted itself into a canteen where the noise level was high enough to drown out the sound of Concorde flying over. The queues were too packed, too intimate. The food was lukewarm and served on plastic plates; the water tumblers were dingy.

Liam opted for something in batter – supposedly fish – a scoop of white chips and a serving of salad that was mostly shredded carrot. He carried his tray from the hatch to the nearest vacant chair. The plan was: shovel food down, get out, find somewhere quiet and try not to think. He kept his eyes on his food and didn't look up until someone sat down opposite him and said, 'Hey, Word Boy!'

Liam raised his head and saw Ben with a pleased-to-see-you smile. He said, 'Hey, Mr Guitar!'

'I hope you're enjoying that delicious and nutritious

meal that our dedicated canteen staff have so carefully prepared,' said Ben. He used a fork to spear one of the chips on his plate and lifted it up. The chip drooped. 'Perfection!' said Ben. He pushed the chip into his mouth and chewed it with extravagant relish.

Liam said, 'I don't know whether to eat this batter, or use it to scratch my name on a window.'

'Leave it, but suck the grease out first,' said Ben.

Liam felt a knot come undone in his stomach. The hall seemed different; the noise receded into the background.

They traded jokes about school dinners, some so old that all the humour had been worn out of them. When they finished eating, they scraped the leftovers into a plastic bin and went outside into the sunshine. The sky was empty except for the scar of a vapour trail. The school looked good: cherry trees in blossom on the front lawn, beds of shrubbery softening the sharp corners of the buildings.

Liam said, 'D'you really want to be a songwriter?'

'*Really* really,' said Ben. 'I want to produce and arrange as well, get my own recording studio. I want to be the guy with the massive headphones, sitting behind the mixing desk.'

'What's a mixing desk?'

Ben caught light. 'It's like this big desk thing, with switches that slide up and down. Each switch controls a recording track. You put every instrument on a different track, and the sliders control how loud they sound when you play back the tape. So, like, the drummer comes in and lays down his bit, then the bass player, then the rhythm and lead guitars, then the vocals. The man on the mixing desk is the one who puts it all together.'

'I didn't know that. I thought bands went into the studio and just did it.'

'Nope. They even have sound mixers with them at live gigs.'

'Know a lot about it, don't you?'

'Only because I'm a sad person with no life. Want to know how sad I am? When I get a new CD or cassette, I read everything on the insert. I memorise the names of the songwriters, the producers, the engineers. Sometimes the inserts tell you what equipment they used – they're my favourite.'

He rambled on about his Porta-Studio, microphones, compressors and delay units. Liam didn't understand any of it, but he liked Ben's enthusiasm. He envied Ben for having something to believe in.

Ben realised he was talking too much and said, 'Whoa! Stop me, somebody, I'm turning into an anorak!'

'No, you're not.'

'D'you play any instruments?' asked Ben.

'No. My mum made me take piano lessons, but I was

hopeless. After three weeks my teacher told Mum she was wasting her money.'

'I had to nag my oldies into letting me take guitar lessons. When I was little, I used to make guitars out of plastic forks, empty matchboxes and rubber bands.'

'You're kidding!'

Ben wasn't; he explained how it was done. 'Music sends shivers down my back. Sometimes when I listen to a piece of music it turns into a movie in my head. When I write a song, I go into this dark place where there's no me, and the song tells me which way it wants to go.'

Liam knew Ben hadn't told many people these things before, because most people would think that he was crazy. He felt like he should give Ben something in return, but he didn't have much. He said, right out of the blue, into a gap in the conversation, 'My parents broke up last Christmas. That's why Mum and I moved here.'

Ben's eyes went serious. 'That's tough. D'you stay in touch with your Dad?'

'He phones. When he's got time. When he remembers.'

'But you don't see him?'

'Not since January. He keeps saying I must come and stay for a weekend, but . . .'

'You don't sound too keen.'

'I'm not.'

Ben understood; it gave Liam a feeling that he couldn't define.

School ended: Liam took a stroll over to the Elgar Block to see if Ben was around, but no luck. Liam headed for home, thinking that things were looking up. The thought didn't last for long.

Billy was at the corner of Dryden Avenue, smoking, giving so-what eyes to the Oxfield Comp pupils who passed him.

Liam saw him, thought about doubling back and finding a way home through the side streets, but Billy clocked him, waved like he was smoothing plaster on to a wall; Liam waved back.

Billy's smile was as twitchy as a dreaming cat's whiskers. 'Lee.'

'Billy.'

Billy didn't hang about, he got stuck straight in with, 'So, what's this I hear about you hanging out with Ben Tollit?'

'Eh?'

'Heard you were with him at lunch-time, having a right old chinwag.'

'Who told you that?'

Billy did a Gestapo-interrogator's voice and said, 'Ve haff shpies everyvere.' He dropped his cigarette and mashed it underfoot. 'What d'you want to talk to that loser for? He's so far round the twist, he's coming back the other way.' Billy cocked a hip, stuck a hand on it, swept back invisible long hair and said, 'All that matters to me is my music!'

Liam laughed. 'Yeah, that's him. He latched on to me at lunch-time and I couldn't get rid of him. I was –' Liam made a cross with his fingers and held it out. 'Stay back, Creature of Darkness! You shall not drink my blood! But he wouldn't take the hint. I wasn't talking to him, he was talking to me. I'll have to have an ear transplant because of him.'

Billy cackled. 'You want to watch yourself round that one, mate. I reckon he's a bit of a shirtlifter on the quiet.'

Liam said, 'Better not stand in front of him in the dinner queue, then.'

Billy mock-punched Liam on the shoulder. 'Coming out tonight?'

'Where?'

'Nowhere. Round.'

Liam said, 'I don't think my mum'll let me.'

'A-a-w! Diddums!'

'It's like, ever since she and Dad split up, she's been keeping tabs on me, you know? She's always fussing. Like, the other night, right, she came up to my bedroom to check if I was OK, because she couldn't hear me moving around. She's all over me.'

'You want to knock that on the head right away. Got to have time for your mates, haven't you?'

'Try telling her that.'

'Just do it. Leave her a note before she gets home from work, go out and don't come back till late. She'll learn.'

'She'd call the police. I'd get grounded for ever.'

'I don't know. Some mums don't ever want their precious little darlings to grow up, do they?'

'Is your mum like that?'

'No way! She doesn't give a toss what I get up to, as long as I don't bring trouble home.'

Billy sounded like he was boasting. Liam didn't know if it was bull, or what. He wondered what Billy really felt about his mum. If you took away Billy's swagger and attitude, what would be left?

Ella's Diary

It is worse now. I didn't think it could get worse, but it always gets worse. The girls in my class are doing it now.

Like this morning I was in registration, and Debbie goes to Linda and Suze, 'Don't forget we got a meeting of the EIP club at break.' She done it loud so's I'd hear.

So I goes, 'What's this EIP club?'

And Debbie goes, 'It's a club what you can't join, Ella. It's a special club, only for me and Linda and Suze.'

So I goes, 'What sort of club is it? What's it mean – EIP? What's it called that name for?'

And they laughed. They all laughed and looked at me.

And then when the bell went, I seen it written on the board.

EIP

ELLA

IS

POOEY

They don't want me in their form. They don't want me around, all fat and slow. They only want pretty girls, clever like them, who wear lots of make-up and that, and talk about boys all the time. Debbie goes out with boys in year nine. Debbie goes round like she thinks she's a supermodel or something.

I don't know now. First it was Billy Pickett and them, and now it's the girls in my class laughing at me. Even when I can't hear them, they're laughing.

The world is getting smaller and smaller.

I am supposed to tell Mrs Lynn if someone says things to me, but I can't go running to her all the time. And anyway, Debbie never really said nothing. It was just in her eyes. I can't take Debbie's eyes to Mrs Lynn. I can't take the way them girls laughed to Mrs Lynn. I don't know if it was them what put the writing on the board.

I got like this pain in my stomach. It's like all the eyes and words and laughing got together and made a pain.

If I didn't have dys I would be clever, and if I didn't have dys I would know what to say back to people when they say things, and they would leave me alone. They still wouldn't like me, but they would leave me alone and that's all I ask.

JUST LEAVE ME ALONE. LEAVE ME ALONE AND SHUT UP, SHUT UP, SHUT UP.

My pen went through the paper. I'm sorry, diary. I didn't mean to hurt you. You're the only friend I got.

You and me got our own club. No one can't join it but us.

It is a club for fat ugly people with dys, what no one else wants.

Ten

Friday morning: double games.

Liam loathed it: the mindless running around, the body contact, having to play as a team. He was uncoordinated. It was as much as he could do to dribble a ball, let alone make a decent pass or score a goal. He never knew what to do with his hands.

The worst part was the showers, those few shaming minutes when you sacrificed your privacy for the team spirit thing. Liam hated the bodies, the jokes, the flicked towels. His nakedness was humiliating, and he rushed out of the showers to escape from it, drying himself so hurriedly that when he got dressed his clothes stuck to the damp places he missed, and his skin felt two sizes too small.

Liam went straight from the changing rooms to the main hall for lunch. Ben was already at a table, eating.

The seat facing him was empty. Liam carried his tray over and sat down; as he did, Ben put a cassette on the table and slid it across. 'Present,' he said.

Liam said, 'What is it?'

Ben said, 'Er, a cassette?'

Liam didn't understand why Ben would want to give him a present. He remembered what Billy had said about Ben being gay. How did you tell stuff like that – and why was it supposed to matter?

'It's the song,' said Ben. 'I did a recording of it.'

Liam picked up the cassette. On the insert was written:

No Way Back
Lyrics/Music: Noakes/Tollit
All instruments and vocals: Ben Tollit
Arranged, Produced and Engineered: Ben Tollit
Recorded at Southey Street Studios.

Liam said, 'Where's Southey Street Studios?'

'My bedroom,' said Ben. 'How about we grab something to eat and then shoot over to the Elgar Block for a listen?' He was keyed-up, eager to share.

'Sure!' Liam pointed at the slice of pizza on his plate. 'Must have looked OK before the truck went over it.'

'Don't eat the crust. It tastes of wall.'

* * *

The vocals were muddied by tape-hiss, the lead guitar fluffed some notes during the solo, but the song had been transformed. Ben had multi-tracked three part harmonies, added sampled bass and strings from a keyboard, and percussion via a drum machine. It ended with Ben repeating, 'No way back,' into a fade out.

Liam was awestruck. The song didn't belong to him and Ben any more, it existed in its own right.

Ben asked, 'What d'you think?'

'Really good,' said Liam. He wished that he could sound as pleased as he felt. He wanted to thank Ben, but he couldn't think of the right way to do it.

Ben said, 'What have you got on tomorrow?'

'Clothes,' said Liam.

Ben clutched his side, pulled a face. 'Ouch! There goes another rib! Seriously, d'you want to get together and have a go at writing something else? I've got a few tunes hanging round, waiting for lyrics.'

Liam hesitated. He knew he was standing on the threshold of a friendship, and that if he crossed it, it would cause problems with Billy.

On the other hand, Ben and Liam had made something that felt important, and Liam wanted the feeling again. He'd put the truth about himself and his parents into what he'd written it was a way for him to say what he could never have said to Mum and Dad face to face.

Ben said, 'Hello? Anyone in?'

'Sorry, I was thinking. Yeah. Tomorrow morning?'

'Guitar lessons.'

'Afternoon?'

'Fine,' said Ben. 'Two o'clock? Meet you outside school. It's not far to my place.'

'You're on,' said Liam.

After lessons were over, Liam went to the school library, got a town map from the reference section and studied it closely, working out a route home that would avoid Billy. He could miss passing Dryden Crescent by going along Wordsworth Road and Coleridge Way, then cut through Keats Lane to the far end of his street. If Billy were waiting outside the house, or if he called, Liam would stonewall him and Just Say No. He had to make the break. It would mean stick from Billy, but Liam had a sharp tongue too; he'd been keeping it in check to stay on-side with Billy, but he could give as good as he got.

All the way home, Liam was thinking about how it would be. He'd wait until Mum was relaxed in the lounge, then he'd play her the tape of the song. She'd instantly know what it was about. She'd finally realise how the games that she and Dad played were tearing Liam apart. It would be a breakthrough: they'd stop using him as a weapon to hurt each other; they'd give him time instead of things and money.

The new route was quicker than the way Liam normally went. To his relief, there was no sign of Billy anywhere, but Mum's car was in the driveway. Mum was never home this early; something must be wrong. Liam hurried.

The house smelled of shower gel and Mum's expensive perfume, the one she kept for special occasions.

'Mum?' Liam called.

'Upstairs, darling. I'm getting ready.'

'What for?'

'Paul's taking me out to dinner, remember? I did tell you.'

Liam jerked as if he'd been punched. His vision of the evening shivered and burst. He went into the lounge and started his homework.

It took Mum an hour and a half to make an appearance. Liam saw that she was going for it: little black dress, high-heeled shoes, dark red nail varnish. She was wearing the necklace that Dad had bought her as an anniversary present; she'd taken off her wedding ring. She said, 'Think I'll do?'

'For what?'

'Paul's driving me up to his favourite restaurant in London. *Very* swish. Am I worth it?' She struck a pose.

'Definitely.'

'There's a Sainsbury's lasagne in the fridge, or you can have a takeaway. I've left you some money on the hall table.'

'What time will you be back?'

'Late, I should think, so don't stay up. I'll try not to make too much noise when I come in.' Mum glanced at her watch. 'He's picking me up at six. The table's booked for eight, but traffic's terrible on a Friday, so we have to leave early. You'll be all right, won't you?'

'I expect so.'

It came out sulkier than Liam had intended, and Mum frowned at him. 'You don't mind, do you?'

'No, but it's not exactly legal to leave someone my age on their own, is it?'

'I know I can trust you to behave responsibly, darling.'

Mum made an effort for other people: she took care over how she looked and made sure she wasn't late. Liam thought that if he weren't around, she'd be like this every night – bubbly, glamorous, a chain of boyfriends whisking her off to dinner, the theatre, the ballet.

What had Mum and Dad been thinking of when they'd decided to have him? What was he for? The only explanation that fitted was that he'd been a mistake: maybe they'd had to get married because Mum was pregnant.

Mum went to the windows and peered out.

Liam said, 'Mum, I met this boy called Ben, at school. He plays the guitar. I helped him to write a song.'

'Did you, darling?' Mum said, without turning round.

'Ben recorded it. Can I play it to you?'

'If you like.'

Liam's hands were shaking as he put the cassette into the tape-drive. He clicked the 'Play' button. Ben's voice filled the room.

Mum listened; there was nothing in her eyes. When the song was over, she said, 'Very nice, darling.'

Liam said, 'I wrote the words, Ben did the music.'

'Well done,' said Mum. She pushed her tongue up under her top lip, then opened her mouth in a wide, ghastly smile. 'I haven't got lipstick on my teeth, have I?'

Paul showed he was keen by arriving ten minutes early. He had a distinguished, young-old face. There were grey streaks in the hair above his ears. He called Liam, 'the man of the house'. 'Thank you for letting me borrow your mother for the evening. I promise to get her back before she turns into a pumpkin.'

'Oh, Liam doesn't mind how late I am, do you, Liam? He's big enough to look after himself, just this once.' Mum leaned forward and kissed the air next to Liam's cheek, so she wouldn't spoil her make-up.

'Have a good time,' said Liam.

He waited at the front door until Paul's black BMW turned the corner, then he went inside and phoned Billy Pickett. Mum definitely wouldn't approve of Billy; Liam needed to do something that Mum wouldn't approve of.

Dusk: shadows seeping out of the walls, street lights gleaming pink, strobing to orange.

Billy and Bing were at the end of Dryden Crescent, the tips of their cigarettes glowing. Billy said, 'Lee! Your Mum let you off the lead, then?'

'We had a barney about it, but I told her straight. Where's Des – late, as usual?'

Billy growled in disgust. 'Not coming, is he? Gone out on a date with Marina Taylor.'

'Marina?' said Liam. 'What are they going to do, water-ski?'

'Des is wasting his time with her,' said Billy. 'She went out with Darryl Crisp, you know, Salt and Vinegar? He said she didn't give anything.'

'Who needs girls?' said Bing. 'Only give you grief, don't they?'

Liam thought of Mum. 'Tell me about it,' he said. 'Where we off to?'

'Down the Parade,' said Billy. 'Get some chips, see what's doing.'

Bing said, 'Shall I nick a nudie mag from the garage, like I did last time?'

'Don't be thick!' said Billy. 'I told you, you don't pull the same stunt in the same place twice. Anyway, the mags they got in the garage are rubbish.'

The Parade was like the back end of nowhere. The chippie was the only bright place in it; the rest of the shops were dark, some sealed behind metal shutters.

Billy, Bing and Liam ate their chips seated on a concrete and wooden bench next to a litter bin. Billy finished his chips, scrunched the greasy paper into a ball and dropped it beside the bin. 'Give the council something to do.' Bing did the same, then let out a window-rattling belch.

'Seven out of ten,' said Billy.

Bing said, 'This sucks. I'm bored. Let's go up the school and break some windows.'

'Good thinking, Bing,' said Billy. 'Shall we wave to the security cameras while we're doing it?'

'Got a better idea?' Bing said resentfully.

'Don't I always?' said Billy. He pulled a phonecard out of the pocket of his bomber jacket. 'Welcome to Wind-Up Time.'

There was a BT phone box in Stevenson Avenue. Billy and Bing piled in, leaving Liam listening at the half-open door.

Billy's first call was to an Indian takeaway. Using a

smooth, well-spoken voice, he ordered ten items and said, 'The name's Lynn. The address is twenty-two, Guildford Road. Yes, that's right. About how long will it be? That's fine. Thank you.' He replaced the receiver. 'Well, that should make Mrs Lynn's Friday night,' he said.

Bing giggled, laughing as he breathed in.

Liam said, 'Was that really Mrs Lynn's address?'

'Course,' said Billy. 'Wouldn't be a proper wind-up otherwise, would it?'

Bing said, 'Ring Ella Thickie, Bill! Go on, ring her!'

Billy said, 'Yeah. Been a while, hasn't it? Time she had a little reminder.'

This time Billy's voice was lighter. He said, 'Oh, hello. Am I speaking to Mr Hickie? British Telecom here. I'm sorry to disturb you, Mr Hickie, but subscribers in your area have been complaining about interference on the line, and we're running tests to see if we can trace the problem. I wonder if you'd mind saying, *I cannot eat my currant bun*? That's right. If you speak as clearly as possible, we'll get a better signal on our equipment. Are you ready?' He held the phone out so that Bing and Liam could hear.

A slow, tinny voice said, 'I cannot eat my currant bun.'

Billy and Bing yelled, 'Stick it up your bum, then!' just before Billy banged down the phone.

Bing's face was red with laughter. 'He probably will, and all!'

Billy's fingers tapped the keys.

'Who are you calling now?' said Liam.

Billy flashed a watermelon-slice grin, then his face went grave. 'Hello?' he said. 'Yeah, fire brigade, quick.' He sounded like he was hyperventilating. 'Hello? There's a fire. Next-door neighbour's house. It looks bad. Oh, yeah, it's at fifteen, Milton Court. The Hickie family. Me? David Brown. I live at number thirteen. I think you'd better hurry.' He hung up.

Bing's laugh turned uncertain, died. 'We going to watch 'em turn up?'

'No,' said Billy. 'We're not going anywhere near the Thickies' house. If Ella clocked us, it'd be a dead giveaway, wouldn't it?'

They walked away from the phone box. Liam was tingling with adrenalin.

Billy said, 'Easy, lads. Just three mates out for a stroll, right? Be cool.'

Three minutes later they heard a fire engine's siren in the distance and saw flashes of blue-white light reflect off the sky.

'Dear, dear, dear!' said Billy. 'I hope that's not my house they're going to.'

Ella's Diary

I don't know what to do no more. It's like everywhere is trouble. It's like everyone got it in for us.

First, Dad come home. He looked awful. He was pale, like he was going to be sick or something. He said, 'They done it. They gave me my cards. Ten years I been there, and now I'm on the scrap heap. What am I going to do? What's going to happen to us?'

So Mum goes, 'Something will turn up, Joe. You'll see. Something always turns up.'

And Dad said, 'Yes, you're right. I'll go down the job centre first thing Monday. They're bound to have something. I'm sure they will.'

But he didn't sound like he believed it. I think he was just saying it so's Mum and me wouldn't feel bad.

I couldn't hardly eat nothing 'cos I was so worried about Dad. I had like a lump in my throat what hurt so I couldn't swallow properly. It wasn't like Friday at all. I like Friday 'cos Dad is all happy about having time off, but he wasn't happy tonight. Even when he was smiling, his eyes were sad.

And then the phone rang, and Dad answered it, and it was kids playing around, and Dad was angry, and then there was all lights and noise, and then this big fire engine come to the house with all firemen, and they were angry, and they like shouted and said they got an emergency call that our house was on fire. We told them and told them that it wasn't us what done it, but it was like they didn't believe us. One of them said they would call the police. I didn't want them to call the police. I was afraid they would take Dad to prison.

In the end the firemen went away. Dad was still angry. He kept going, 'If I find out who done it, I'll knock their blocks off.'

And Mum said, 'Calm down, Joe. It was just kids mucking round.'

I know what kids. I know it was Billy Pickett and them, but I won't say nothing 'cos I don't want Dad going round Billy Pickett's house and getting into trouble.

Why they doing this to us? What they want to do it for? For a laugh? For a joke?

SO, BIG JOKE, BILLY PICKETT. HA HA HA.

Nanna used to say the darkest hour is just before the dawn, but this is all dark and no dawn.

What they going to do next? It used to be just me at school, *but now it's Mum and Dad as well.*

The house knows. It feels different. It feels nervous, like it's waiting for the next thing to happen. It doesn't feel like home no more. It feels like an eggshell someone is going to step on so's it breaks into thousands of pieces, and no one won't be able to put it back together again, like Humpty Dumpty.

There is nowhere to hide, nowhere to go. I can't get away now. It's always going to be like this, for ever and ever. It's always going to be the same. The names. The phone. No matter where I go, I will always be me. It's my fault. They'll always get at me because I got dys and glandular, and I can't learn nothing as fast as what they can. They only like see the outside. That's all what anybody sees, just what you look like. They can't see inside to the bit that really matters. They just look and go like, 'Oh, she's fat, she's ugly, she's thick.' When you got those names they're like burnt on your skin and you can't never wash them off. People see the names when they look at you. They don't see I'm Ella.

I can't curl safe up in bed no more. I can hear the house listening for people creeping round. The monsters aren't in my dreams no more. The monsters come to life and they are walking round in the night. If they were still in my dreams, I could wake up and they would be gone. But how can you wake up when you're not asleep?

How can you make the monsters go away when they are really there?

Eleven

On Saturday morning, Mum looked as if she were paying for Friday night. There were lilac circles under her eyes. Her hair was dry and straggly. She walked around in a mist, frowning at things like they didn't make sense.

Liam didn't talk to her until she'd finished her second cup of black coffee. 'Did you enjoy yourself last night?'

Mum smiled, winced, said, 'Mm.'

'How was the restaurant?'

'Fine.'

Liam wriggled in his chair. He had something to say that he'd been putting off for a week, hoping to find the right moment; but there wasn't going to be a right moment. He said, 'When Dad rang last Sunday to tell me about Mia, he said he wanted me to go and stay with him one weekend.'

Mum withdrew, became defensive. 'When?'

'I don't know. Next month. He's going to ring and tell me.'

'Oh, so he's remembered he's got a son, then?'

Dad wasn't there; Liam had to take the sarcasm for him.

'The only thing is, I'm not sure I want to go.'

Mum blinked at him. 'Why not?'

'I don't know. I don't think I'd feel, you know . . . comfortable.'

'But you mustn't feel like that. We explained it to you. We're all adjusting to the new situation, Liam. You're not the only one who finds it hard. It's no use burying your head in the sand.'

'I know. I'm not. I just don't feel ready yet. Being with Dad and Mia would be too embarrassing.'

The caffeine kicked in; Mum's brain started to function. Her voice became gently insistent. 'You'll have to face them at some point. The longer you leave it, the more difficult it's going to be.'

Liam thought he had enough difficulties to be going on with, without adding a weekend with Dad to the heap.

'Besides, when you're with someone all the time, seeing them every day – I mean, when it's –' Mum sighed. 'I don't want you to take this the wrong way, darling, but there are times when I feel that I need my own space. It does people good to take an occasional break from each other. It stops them taking each other for granted.'

Mum hadn't wanted Liam to take it the wrong way; he wondered what the right way might be.

Mum laughed and said, 'Oh, dear! I don't think I put that very well. I didn't mean it to sound as if I didn't want you here.'

Oh no? Liam thought.

'But it is important for you to have contact with your father. There's only so much I can do. He can give you things that I can't, give you a different view of things, broaden your perspective.'

She sounded like the family counsellor that they'd had sessions with.

What it came down to was that Mum was telling Liam he was going to stay with Dad whether Liam wanted to or not. When she talked about her own space, she meant freedom. With Liam out of the way she could go out with Paul – or whoever – invite him over for dinner: candlelight, wine, smoochy jazz on the stereo. It was all in her eyes.

'You do understand, don't you, darling?'

Liam said, 'Yes.'

How could he ever have been so dumb as to think that a song would help him explain things to his parents? If he etched his feelings on a bullet and fired it at them, it would bounce off. All they needed from him was his absence. He was a miscalculation, a walking reminder of where they'd gone wrong.

Liam rang Ben's number and got the answering machine. He said, 'Ben, it's Liam. Can't make it this afternoon, something's come up. See you round school next week.'

He hoped that Ben would be disappointed; he needed someone else to feel the same way he did. Mum and Dad didn't want him, he could see that now, so he had to find a way of showing that he didn't want them. What did they care whether he was writing songs with Ben, or goofing off with Billy Pickett and the lads?

He was on his own; no one was bothered what he did.

This time Liam waited for Billy at the bus stop on Betjeman Street. Billy arrived with Bing, and the three of them went into the town centre together. No one was sure if Des was coming: Billy said if he didn't turn up by two, they'd split.

It was a clone of the previous Saturday – same crowded market, same alkies in the churchyard.

Bing said, 'Great laugh last night, wasn't it? Wonder what the Thickies said when the fire engine came?'

Billy made his face gormless, clouded his eyes; he pointed at nothing. In a rumbling, scarcely-human voice he said, 'Ooh, El-la! Look, it's a fi-re engine!'

Liam picked it up. 'But there ain't no fi-re, Dad!'

'Ooh! We bet-ter start one, then!' Billy mimed pouring a can of petrol over Liam and setting it alight. He made the WHOOF! sound of the petrol igniting, and held his hands out to the warmth of the imaginary blaze. 'Ooh! Sor-ry, El-la! But it's chea-per than cen-tral heat-ing!'

Liam laughed. The Thickies were brilliant: they were a cartoon series, a set of recurring characters in a TV comedy, like the *Fast Show*. They did incredibly stupid things without realising that they were stupid. You could blow them up, drop ten-ton weights on their heads and they'd pop back into shape every time.

Billy said, 'Giss a fag, Bing.'

'Can't,' said Bing. 'Haven't got any. Didn't get any pocket money this week, did I? Old man spent it down the pub.'

'You poor, deprived child!' said Billy. He fished out his own packet, removed a cigarette and tossed it to Bing. 'There you go.'

Billy and Bing lit up. Billy blew out smoke, then crooked a finger at Liam and Bing to draw them into a huddle. There were secrets in his face; he lowered his voice and said, 'Might be scoring tonight. Seven quid deal. Supposed to be wicked gear.'

'Off of who?' said Bing.

Billy said, 'What you don't know can't hurt you. In your case, Bing, that means nothing can hurt you.'

Liam didn't follow, until Billy said, 'Ever done blow, Lee?'

'Huh?'

'You know,' said Billy, 'dope, hash.'

'No. Never got the chance.'

Billy made a dreamy face. 'You are missing something, mate!' he said.

'It's the best,' said Bing.

Liam's brain went: *Danger! Danger! This is drugs! This is flat-eyed guys sticking dirty hypodermics in their arms! This is what everybody tells you not to do!*

Des arrived. He was wearing black tracksuit bottoms and a hooded grey top. He looked like a boxer in training.

'So there you are, lover boy,' said Billy. 'Thought you might be worn out after last night. How'd it go?'

Des smiled shyly, ducked his head. 'OK. Marina's all right, you know?'

Billy leered, waggled his tongue.

'Nah, it wasn't like that. We went to see this movie and then we talked about it on the way back. Marina's a top girl.'

Billy scalded him with a glance. 'Girls are only good for one thing, and if they don't give it, they're a waste of space.'

Des looked like he didn't agree, but he knew when to keep his mouth shut.

Virgin again; the mall again – no bus-number victims this week; the market again; McDonald's again. Liam took pity on Bing and subbed him for a Big Mac. Billy scoffed his burger in record time, then started pinching Liam's fries.

Billy said, 'Gonna be fun tonight.'

'Yeah?' said Des. 'How come?'

Billy said, 'Gonna get a lit-tle bit out of it, and then . . .' He reached inside his bomber jacket and brought out a can of aerosol paint.

'Where d'you get that?' said Bing.

Billy said, 'Nicked it off a stall in the market, didn't I?'

'I never saw you do it,' said Bing.

'Bing,' Billy said slowly, 'that's how you're supposed to nick stuff – so no one sees you.'

'What's it for?' said Liam.

Billy told him: he had it all worked out, times, places, who was going to do what. He spun the details into a web; the others flew straight into it.

Mum was on the phone when Liam came in. As he opened the door, she said, 'Must go!' and fumbled replacing the receiver. She turned to Liam with a bright, phoney smile. 'Hello, darling! Did you have a good time with your friends?'

'Uh-hu.'

'There was a call for you. Ben, I think it was. He wants you to ring him back when you get a chance.'

'Will do. Mum, my friends are going to the cinema tonight. Can I go with them?'

Mum looked suspicious. 'What's the film?'

'That new science fiction movie.'

'It's not violent, is it? I don't want you seeing films with too much violence in them.'

'It's a comedy. All the kids at school have been talking about it. They say it's brilliant.'

Liam was playing: if-you-say-no-I'll-be-the-odd-one-out.

Mum's eyes were vacant. She was thinking about something else – someone else. She smiled without knowing that she was doing it. 'All right. But I want you back by ten-thirty. No later.'

'Thanks, Mum.'

'And don't hang around after the film. Come straight home.'

'I will,' said Liam. He'd got what he wanted, and from the look on her face, so had Mum; they were even.

At nine o'clock, Billy, Des, Bing and Liam were hidden in

a clump of birch trees that grew on a triangle of undeveloped land at the junction of Milton Court and Tennyson Gardens. The triangle was a token piece of green belt: grass, brambles, gorse, bracken. It had just been left, a tiny island of what had been there before the estates were built. It smelled of earth, damp leaves; the ground was scattered with wrappers and flattened cans.

From the trees there was a view across the road to number fifteen, the Thickies' house, but no one was looking. All eyes were on Billy as he thumbed a plastic lighter into flame and lit the spliff that he'd rolled. Liam had the same, illicit feeling he used to get as a kid when he played around with fireworks – using elastic bands to tie a banger on to the stick of a rocket so it exploded in mid-flight; letting off a banger under the arch of a railway bridge. The thrill came from breaking the rules: small-time wild side.

Billy drew down smoke and held it in for almost a minute before letting it out. 'G-o-o-d!' he said. His voice was hoarse.

Des said, 'It de 'oly 'erb, mon!'

Billy took a second drag, then offered the spliff to Liam. 'Wrap your laughing tackle around that.'

'What do I do?' said Liam.

Billy said, 'Get a mouthful of smoke, right? Then breathe it in, hold it so the blow gets into your bloodstream and breathe out.'

Liam felt stupid, like he was imitating a movie hard-man.

He was breathing bonfire smoke; his lungs were being sandpapered; he spluttered.

'Keep it in, Lee!' Billy snapped. 'That's my money you're wasting there.'

Liam held the smoke in, breathed out, wiped his watering eyes.

Billy said, 'Take another hit.'

Second time wasn't as bad, but Liam coughed as he exhaled. He passed the spliff to Des.

The spliff went round twice more. Liam noticed that Billy, Des and Bing had happy eyes and wondered if his looked the same. Des said, 'You know that thing where you get in the bath, and it goes all over you, and there's like a spring in your head?'

'Yeah?' said Billy.

'Er . . . I forget,' said Des.

Bing laughed, wheezing like a kettle on the point of boiling. The laugh stuttered to a halt, then came back stronger.

'What's so funny?' said Billy.

'No idea, mate!' said Bing.

'You're stoned,' Billy said. 'Get anything off it, Lee?'

Liam said, 'Not sure. I don't think –'

It came in a wave, stopping him in mid-sentence. He looked out through the trees to the houses and street lights, and the black sky behind them. It was strange: the lights were aliens, craning their spindly necks to peer down at the road; the houses had faces, windows for eyes, doors for mouths . . .

'He's on one!' said Des, patting Liam's shoulder. 'Cool, eh?'

Liam didn't know: he wanted things to return to normal; the back of his head was getting longer.

Bing was still laughing; his face was like a wax mask.

Billy said, 'Knock it off, Bing! Someone's coming!'

Footsteps.

Liam was scared. It was the police; he was going to get caught; he could already feel the vinyl upholstery of the squad car give as he sat in it; policemen talking into radios; Mum's shocked face.

A man walked by, with a dog on a lead. The dog stopped at a streetlight, sniffed, cocked its leg.

'Come on!' the man said.

Footsteps; getting quieter; going to nothing.

Billy said, 'No one else about. Let's do it.'

'What if someone comes?' said Liam.

'We leg it,' said Billy. 'Meet up down the Parade. Now move it!'

They spread out through the trees. Des squatted

behind a gorse bush, Bing took cover in a clump of bracken. Billy went out into the open, creeping like a shadow on a wall. He crossed the road, paused at the front gate of number fifteen, opened it noiselessly and went up the front path. He took out the aerosol can, sprayed THICKIE across the front door, pushed the doorbell and came flying back across the road as if he'd been thrown. He made the trees just as the door opened.

A big man looked out, a man shaped like one of those round-bottomed dolls that flips up every time it's knocked over. He caught sight of the writing on the door and gasped. Liam heard him say, 'What the –?'

Billy called out, 'Oh, Mr Thick-ie! Oh, Mr Thick-ie!' His voice rose and fell to the tune of the old playground taunt.

The man stepped onto the path. 'Who's that?' he said. 'Who's there?'

Des's voice came from Liam's right. 'Fat man in yo' garden! Fat man in yo' garden!'

The man's head snapped around.

Bing hooted, 'Ella-Ella-Ella, ooh! Ella-Ella-Ella, ooh!'

The man's head turned the other way. He waddled clumsily to the gate. 'Who's there?' he shouted.

Liam yelled, 'Tree-trunk, tree-trunk legs! Tree-trunk, tree-trunk legs!'

The man's head moved this way and that.

The chanting went on and on.

A curtain moved in one of the house's upstairs windows. Liam saw a pale, round face.

They all chanted, 'Ella-Ella-Ella, ooh! Ella-Ella-Ella, ooh! Ella, ooh!'

Mr Hickie stood at the gate. His eyes were bewildered, like the eyes of an animal in a snare, not understanding where the pain was coming from, or why it couldn't move.

'Ella-Ella-Ella, ooh! Ella-Ella-Ella, ooh! Ella, ooh!'

Mr Hickie roared wordlessly.

The despair in the voice made something in Liam crack open and fall away. He stopped chanting. It wasn't one of the Thickies, it was Mr Hickie, Ella's father, and he was real. What was Liam doing hiding here, watching someone he didn't know being tormented by people he didn't like? He didn't want to be one of them; that wasn't who he was. They were kids shrivelling ants with a magnifying glass, pelting cats with stones, shooting sparrows with air rifles. They enjoyed torturing things that were weaker than they were; it made them feel powerful. And he was with them: Nice Boy Liam, Clever Liam, Sensitive Liam.

Then time went too fast for Liam to follow, and so slowly that he took in every detail.

Ella came out of the house, screaming, 'Stop it! Leave me alone, leave me alone!' She ran down the path, shouldered her way past her father, went across the pavement and into the road.

Liam saw the headlights of an approaching car, heard the sound of the engine getting louder and knew what was going to happen. He stood up and shouted, 'Look out!'

Ella kept on running, blinded by tears.

The car braked, tyres squealing and smoking. There was a hollow thud, like an axe striking a log, and Ella spun through the air.

Mr Hickie shouted, 'Oh, God! Ella!'

Liam ran. Thorns tore at his clothes, a birch twig lashed his face. He ran into the strangeness of the street, the world tipping and yawing like a plate wobbling on top of a juggler's stick.

He threw up onto a drain cover in Wordsworth Road, fighting for breath as the remains of his last meal plopped through the gaps in the grating. He was crying, thinking, What if she's dead? He was afraid and ashamed: he'd betrayed himself and helped to cause an accident – and for what? To score points with Billy Pickett? To get back at Mum and Dad? He wished he'd never come to this town, never gone to Oxfield Comp, never met Billy Pickett.

He wished that he could be someone else.

Twelve

Liam spent the morning hoping the world would go away. He'd told Mum that he'd eaten a dodgy hot-dog at the cinema and it had upset his stomach, so she left him alone. He drifted in and out of sleep, but his dreams were almost as bad as being awake, and at lunch-time he gave up, got out of bed and went downstairs.

Mum was in the lounge, reading through the business section of one of the big Sundays. She looked up from the newspaper as Liam came in, and said, 'How's the tummy?'

'Iffy,' said Liam.

'Would you like something to eat?'

'Maybe later.'

Mum said, 'Liam, you and your friends weren't drinking last night, were you?'

'No.'

'Is that the truth?'

Liam said, 'It was the hot-dog.'

'Only, I know how it can be when young lads get together. They egg one another on. They make people do things they normally wouldn't, to stay in with the group.'

Like, *now* she was telling him.

'But I know you're too intelligent to be taken in by all that macho nonsense. You've been brought up to think for yourself. You don't have a mob mentality.'

Liam was going to tell her: he wanted to see her face when she found out how wrong she was about him. He was just as irresponsible as anyone his age; he was no better than anybody else. He said, 'No, you're –'

The phone rang.

Mum said, 'I'll go. You look like you need to sit down.' She went into the hall, answered in her telephone voice, came back into the lounge and said, 'It's for you, darling. It's Billy.'

Liam's insides coiled like a snake. He didn't want to talk to Billy, but he had to; he had to say: *That's it. No more. I don't want to know you.* He found a hot coal of anger and carried it to the phone.

Billy said, 'You heard?'

'What?'

Billy said, 'Ella Thickie's in hospital. It was on local

radio news. Broke her leg, stupid cow!' He was being cocky, hard-boiled.

Liam went cold with relief. 'She's going to be all right, isn't she?' he said.

Billy laughed. 'Take a tank to flatten her, wouldn't it? Bet that car's a complete write-off.' Billy lowered his voice. 'Listen, Lee, about last night. We didn't see each other, right? Just in case anybody asks.'

'Like who?' said Liam.

'I don't know, somebody might, that's all. Don't think they will, mind. Nobody knows we were round the Thickies', do they?'

'We do,' said Liam.

'Then we'd better forget about it, hadn't we? As long as we keep quiet, there's nothing to worry about.'

'But . . . Ella's in hospital,' said Liam.

'Yeah, but it's nothing to do with us. We didn't know she was going to run out in the road like that, did we? We didn't know she'd go mental. We were only having a laugh. Least said, soonest mended, I reckon.'

Liam wasn't sure: he knew that more than Ella's leg had been broken, and broken in a way that couldn't mend.

At three o'clock the door bell rang. Liam went to answer it, and it was Ben. Ben didn't smile. He looked part offended, part let-down. He said, 'So where were you on Saturday? Why didn't you get back to me?'

'I had to go out,' said Liam.

'And you couldn't spare two minutes to phone me?' Ben stopped, saw deeper into Liam's eyes and said, 'Hey, what's up? What's happened?'

'Something awful,' said Liam. 'Can you come in for a talk?'

'Sure.'

Up in his bedroom, Liam found that once he'd started, he couldn't leave anything out, and he spilled the lot: Mum and Dad, getting in with Billy, the phone calls, the name-calling, the accident.

Ben listened without comment, and said finally, 'Jeez, Liam! When you bodge-up, you don't go halfway, do you? How could you be so dumb?'

Liam said, 'Because I'm spoilt, and selfish, and stupid, and I didn't think.'

Ben didn't say anything to contradict him.

Liam said, 'What if Ella knows who it was, Ben? What if she tells anybody? What will I do?'

'Take it,' said Ben. 'And if she doesn't tell anybody, you ought to.'

'And get my head kicked in by Billy, Des and Bing?'

'If you don't say anything, Billy's always going to have something on you – and don't think he won't use it. He's a control-freak. He'll stitch you up just for laughs.'

Liam hadn't thought about that, but he did now.

'I wouldn't want that slimeball to have any kind of hold over me, but it's not down to me, is it? You're the one who has to live with yourself.' Ben glanced at his watch. 'I have to go. I told Mum and Dad I'd only be an hour.'

'OK. Ben, are we still friends?' Of all the difficult things Liam had said, it was the most difficult, because it sounded so pathetic.

'I heard you out, didn't I? I'm not on the phone to the police, am I?'

'Wouldn't blame you if you were.'

Ben sighed. 'If you think you deserve to be punished, you're going to have to do something about it yourself. Don't expect me to do it for you.'

Liam dreaded going to school on Monday morning. He was certain that there'd be a special year eight assembly, and that Mrs Lynn would call out him, Billy, Des and Bing in front of everybody. They'd all be permanently excluded, maybe face police charges. Liam figured he had it coming. He'd made fun of Ella Thickie the cartoon character, and taken the joke way too far. By the time he'd realised that Ella was a person, it had been too late. Now he knew that some jokes weren't funny – they were a way of turning people into things and he loathed himself for joining in with them.

But nothing happened: no special assembly, no public shaming. Some kids mentioned the accident, and most of them made cracks about the car bouncing off Ella, or getting stuck between her bum-cheeks so that she'd had to go to hospital to get it removed.

Billy was chuffed. After registration, he grabbed Liam in the corridor and said, 'Knew we'd have nothing to worry about. Ella's too thick to know it was us, and even if she did she wouldn't dare grass us up. We're in the clear, mate!' He didn't care that Ella was in hospital, or that she might be crippled for life; all Billy cared about was getting away with it. 'Hey, Lee!' he said. 'I'm bunking off at lunch-time, find a quiet place to finish off that blow. Coming?'

'No,' said Liam.

Billy scowled at the tone in Liam's voice. 'What's up with you?' he said.

Liam said, 'I'm meeting Ben Tollit at lunch-time.'

'What for? Fancy a bit of the other, do you?'

'We write songs together.'

'Songs?' said Billy. 'Ooh, darling! How romantic!'

Anger got the better of Liam's mouth. 'You know what, Billy? I feel sorry for you.'

'Oh? Why's that then?'

'Because you're so sad.'

Billy's eyes went dangerous. 'Shut it! No one talks to me like that, right? Just remember, I can get you up to your neck in it any time I want, no sweat.'

'You don't scare me.'

'No? Don't I?'

Billy didn't scare Liam, but what Billy knew did. Liam turned and walked away.

'Lily!' Billy called out after him. 'Oi, Lil! Have a good time with Ben Toilet. Kissy-kissy, sweetheart!'

And Liam knew he was going to be punished, but not by the school or the police. Billy was finished with Ella – now it was Liam's turn.

On Friday after school, Liam had tea at Ben's house. Ben's house was warm and chaotic. His mother rushed at everything, dropping stuff, spilling fruit juice on the tablecloth and generally panicking. Ben had two younger sisters: five year old Becca, who kept burping and laughing, and eight year old Anne, who went red whenever she looked at Liam. Every time Anne blushed, Becca yelled, 'Ann-ie's in lo-ove! Ann-ie's in lo-ove!'

Above the ensuing row, Mrs Tollit said, 'I'm sorry, Liam! I don't know what you must think of us.'

'It was kind of you to invite me, Mrs Tollit.'

He couldn't tell her what he actually thought: that it

was great; mad and messy, the way a home ought to be. He envied Ben his mother and sisters. They made fun of one another, snapped at one another. Nobody pretended anything. And when Mr Tollit came home, and his daughters ran shrieking to wrap themselves around him, like professional wrestlers going into a clinch, Liam envied that too.

Later, in the recording-studio/bedroom, Ben and Liam wrote a song from scratch, words and music arriving simultaneously.

Grey skies, rain eyes,
No one seems to care,
No one knows you're there,
Sees how hard you try,
Hears how hard you cry.

Grey skies, rain eyes,
Nowhere you can hide
From the pain inside.
How much can you take
Till you start to break?

Grey skies, rain eyes,
If they only knew
What they've done to you.

How their cruel lies
Gave you rainy eyes.

Ben put down his guitar and said, 'That's about Ella Hickie, isn't it?'

Liam nodded.

Ben said, 'If you can tell it in a song, you can tell her.'

'*What?*'

'You ought to go and see her in hospital, tell her you're sorry.'

'She'd freak! She'd call me all the names under the sun!'

'So?' said Ben. 'Look what you did to her.'

Liam shook his head. 'I couldn't, Ben! I couldn't face her.'

Ben put on a voice that made him sound like Grandpa Walton. 'Son,' he said, 'there comes a time in a boy's life when he has to start learning how to be a man. I reckon you've reached that time.'

'You're right.'

'The hell I am, boy!'

'No. I'm not joking. I mean it.' Liam smiled unsteadily. 'I didn't know growing up was going to be like this,' he said.

'Like what?'

'So scary. If I do go to the hospital, will you come with me?'

'No chance! Grown ups do things on their own. They're not afraid of the dark.'

'Oh, cheers, mate! Thanks for making it easy for me!'

'You don't need it to be easy,' said Ben. 'You just need to do it.'

And he was right again.

Liam put it off for a week, waiting for the right moment, then worked out that the right moment wasn't something that arrived, it was something he had to make. He went straight from school to the hospital on Thursday afternoon, bought a bunch of flowers from a stall in the hospital carpark and went in through the main entrance, convinced that it was all happening to someone else. A receptionist at the enquiry desk told him what ward Ella was on, and how to get there. Liam crossed the foyer to the lifts and pressed the 'Up' button.

The lift pinged, the doors slid open and Liam stepped inside, thinking that if this was such a good idea, how come he was so frightened?

Epilogue

Ella had said that she wanted Liam to understand, and when he finished reading her diary, he did. He also understood what he'd done, in a way that left him no excuses and no place to hide. 'I'm sorry' wouldn't do it, he had to show Ella, make it up to her – try to salvage some self-respect.

But how?

Liam went down to breakfast on Friday morning and caught Mum in the middle of her tornado-act. 'I'm not sure what time I'll be home this evening, darling. If I'm not back by eight, phone for a takeaway or something. All right?'

Liam said, 'Actually, no it isn't.'

Mum froze, mouth open. 'Sorry?'

'Can't you come home early? I have to talk to you about something.'

'What is it?'

Liam shut his eyes so he couldn't see Mum's face. 'I can't explain now. I can't squash it into a couple of minutes. I need your time.'

'But I can't drop things just like that, Liam. People are depending on me.'

Liam looked at her. 'Mum,' he said, '*I'm* depending on you.'

What Mum saw in Liam's eyes melted her. 'I haven't been fair to you, have I? I've been so wrapped up in the new job that –' She paused. 'No!' she said. 'Stop making excuses and *do* something, right?'

'Please.'

Mum's eyes went from side to side as she ran through mental checklists. 'Fine,' she said. 'I'll be home by half-past four. I'm not going to promise, I'm going to do it.'

'Thanks.'

'But I wish you'd tell me now.'

Liam couldn't; he didn't know what he'd have to tell. 'Not yet.'

'Is it something at school, or –?'

'Not yet,' Liam said again.

It was blatant emotional blackmail, and it wasn't very mature, but Liam didn't feel mature. He wanted to shrink until he was small enough for Mum to pick him up, and cuddle him, and tell him that everything was all right.

'I do care about you, Liam. I don't say it often enough, I know, but . . .' Liam was expecting the usual stuff about having a career and being a single parent; instead, Mum said, 'After all we've been through, all the changes . . . I'm still trying to work out who I am.'

'Me too,' Liam said.

Liam took Ella's diary to school with him. All the way there he could feel the diary in his bag, like an extra weight. The memory of what he'd read stayed with him, made him see Oxfield Comp the way that Ella did: a hostile place, full of snares and emotional landmines – especially outside Shakespeare Block with the rest of Eight Luke West, waiting for Mr Cooper. Liam turned himself off, in preparation for the morning confrontation with Billy.

Billy had it down to a slick routine, nudging Des and Bing as Liam approached, then blowing Liam a kiss and saying, 'Morning, Lily!'

Des and Bing giggled, waiting for Billy's latest joke, which he told out of the side of his mouth while staring straight at Liam. Liam held Billy's stare, not feeling frightened or angry.

Billy's joke ended with a petulant pout and a wiggle of his hips. Des and Bing cracked up; Billy didn't laugh or smile, his eyes fixed on Liam's, like they were two gunslingers in a dusty street, facing-off at high noon.

Liam thought, Go ahead, Billy! It's not going to work. You're not going to get to me, because I *know* about you.

He'd learned it from Ella's diary: people made jokes about what they were frightened of in themselves – the things that made them feel inadequate, or different. The jokes made out that there was something wrong with being gay, or black, or overweight, or thin, or brilliant, or disadvantaged, or whatever. Laughing was a way of showing that you weren't like that, that you fitted-in.

To have jokes made against you, all you had to do was be born.

It rained at lunch-time. Liam sat in one of the practice rooms in Elgar Block with Ben, and showed him Ella's diary, reading bits out loud. He felt uneasy about it, like he was betraying Ella's trust by showing her diary to someone else, but Liam thought that if Ella knew Ben, she wouldn't mind.

Ben said, 'Makes you think, doesn't it? Like normally you think of bullies as those guys in comics, you know? The beefy thug holding the weedy swot upside-down, shaking money from his pockets? Teachers can spot stuff like that a mile off and put a stop to it. But Billy goes in for invisible bullying.'

'The kind that leaves the bruises on the inside,' said Liam.

Ben said, 'Who'll be next?'

'Huh?'

'Ella's in hospital, so Billy can't pick on her for the moment. Who's he got lined up as his next victim?'

Liam said, 'Er, well . . .' and he told Ben some of the things that Billy had been saying about them.

Ben's face reddened with anger. 'I'd really like to stick one on that kid!' he said.

'You'd have to go through Bing first,' Liam pointed out.

Ben flexed the muscles in his arms and laughed. 'Yeah!' he said. 'Not exactly the action-hero type, am I?'

There was a silence that lasted long enough for Liam to register the sound of rain on the windows, then Ben said, 'You can stop Billy.'

'I can?'

'Talk to your form tutor,' said Ben. 'Show him the diary. Tell him what happened – what's happening.'

'Blow the whistle on Billy, Des and Bing?'

'And yourself,' Ben said.

Liam considered it. He'd be breaking the most sacred unwritten school rule: *Thou shalt not grass-up another pupil to a teacher*. He'd have to tell Mum and Dad; the head might sling him out of school.

But . . .

Liam imagined thousands of schools, each with its own Ella Hickie and Billy Pickett, each with its own crowd of witnesses who looked on and said nothing.

And the real crime was the silence: it was what made the bullying possible.

When Mr Cooper was told that a pupil wanted to see him, he wasn't pleased. Friday was his Duty Day, and he'd spent most of the lunch-break Rottweilering noisy kids who'd been forced into their form rooms by the rain, and denied the chance of burning off their excess energy outside. He was left with fifteen minutes to gulp down a salad roll and a cup of tea, and psych himself up for the afternoon session.

As he made his way to the door of the staff room, Mr Cooper thought for about the thousandth time, If it weren't for the kids and the parents and the other staff, teaching would be a halfway decent job!

But when he got out into the corridor, Mr Cooper's annoyance vanished as soon as he saw Liam's and Ben's faces. He noticed that Liam was clutching a book that had a picture of a puppy on its front cover.

'What's this – a delegation?' said Mr Cooper.

Liam was trembling. He took a breath to steady his voice, and said, 'Sir, can I have a word with you?'